Strange Sands Suspense 5
Beaufort

I0544106

The Devil's Drawer

Pamela Poole

Southern Sky Publishing

Southern Sky Publishing
southernskypublishing.com

Cover image created with the help of Craiyon online tools.
Cover created in BookBrush

eBook ISBN: 978-1-956089-26-4
Print ISBN: 978-1-956089-27-1
Print ISBN: 978-1-956089-28-8

Author's Note

Have you ever walked into a place and instantly became ill at ease? Did you ever meet someone, and your spirit clashed with his or hers? Was there ever a time when you couldn't explain it, but you simply knew something bad might happen at any moment—and it did?

The novellas in the Strange Sands Suspense series will follow the adventures of a young lady named Mercedes Ellison, whose family has a long history of unexplainable encounters that many would call "strange." But then, Christians are peculiar people who should be living supernatural lives. To grow in our faith is to be uncomfortable. Modern Christianity has sanitized the supernatural, even though it fills Scripture.

The stories and people in this series are fictional, but they are steeped in places I've been, situations I've experienced, true stories of friends and acquaintances, and people I interviewed who have had these encounters—encounters they typically keep to themselves. Each story will contain at least one of these.

I hope you'll enjoy the Southern Lowcountry ambiance in this series, where moments spent on warm sandy beaches blend with the grains of strange sand slipping through history's hourglass.

"I warn you against shedding blood,
indulging in it and making it a habit,
for blood never sleeps."
Ayyubid Sultan Salah ad-Din (Saladin)
To his sons before his death

Chapter 1

"Leave the key in the lock," growled a rough voice from an even rougher looking man dressed all in black and blending into the night. He grunted as he silently lifted a well-oiled hand truck over a threshold blanketed with a furniture cover.

Behind him, another man in black with a black knit cap kept his voice low as he rasped, "Oh, that's right. Almost forgot. Doesn't make sense, though."

He closed a heavy wood front door silently and inserted a black key in the lock. The key seemed to disappear in the darkness of a hot, humid evening, and the other man mumbled that nothing made sense with the people who hired them.

Two more men were in the back of a delivery truck in the driveway, folding up furniture covers with several mysterious symbols on them. The man with the last hand truck rolled it silently over more furniture pads on the sidewalk, then to the back of the truck. Behind him, the last man rolled up the furniture pads and looked everywhere to be sure they had left no trace of their presence.

As he turned to join the delivery crew in the truck, he muttered, "Pretty sure nobody ordered that thing for this house."

"Could there be a more gorgeous day?"

Mercedes Ellison flung these joyful words toward the landscape sunroof as she prayed whatever popped into her mind, following the highway to beautiful Beaufort, South

Carolina. "Thank you, Jesus, for days like this. Thank you for letting me live and work in the Lowcountry."

The cloudless blue sky over sparkling water and wildlife-filled salt marshes pushed away the sad mist around her heart. When she left her summer cottage in Bluffton this morning to meet a new client, her mind was still on the funeral for her last client's brother. The strange circumstances that unfolded the previous week were only the latest she had experienced in what she had imagined would be a relaxing summer.

This was a new day, a fresh beginning. She had assured her fiancé, Quincy, that as far as she could tell, there were no surprises about this job for filing paperwork on Seashell Cottage. Remembering his quip that she thought that about every client, she laughed out loud.

The diamond ring on her finger flashed in the glorious sunshine as her hand rested on the steering wheel, bringing a smile to her face. Glancing down at the new outfit her mother had bought for her last week while they shopped at the boutiques on Hilton Head Island, she remembered the extra clothes she packed in a tote bag to change into later that afternoon, when her appointment was over. It would be another hot day in the Lowcountry, and she wanted to be comfortable walking around the shops and galleries near the waterfront park. She exhaled a long sigh of contentment as she thought of sitting on a swing in the shade of an old oak dripping with Spanish moss, watching the lazy boats drifting into the marina. She would enjoy watching the creative names printed on them while she was eating her picnic lunch. Then she might make a few sketches of the boats. Perhaps the Prince of Tides boat would be among them, and if she ever did a painting of it, the subject would be popular here in the town who claimed author Pat Conroy as its own.

The soothing voice on her Jeep's navigation screen guided her into a wonderful historic area off the beaten path of tourism. She appreciated the views of sprawling, moss-draped oaks, sidewalks like patched, crooked spines with spider veins, and walls and fences that sheltered aging gardens. Historic churches and their quaint cemeteries crept by while her vehicle's navigation assured her the destination was ahead on the right.

The driveway of Seashell Cottage was laid in pavers and crushed seashells. Mercedes slowly followed it, surrounded by the varied colors and textures of the flower blooms in the front yard. The lawn, hedges, flower beds, and paths were lovingly tended, providing beautiful views from inside the welcoming windows. From the outside, those windows reflected blue sky, magnolia blooms, and the crooked oak limbs.

There was no other car waiting. She parked close to the walkway, then started gathering what she would need to show her client and to take notes about the house.

Before tucking her cell phone away, she checked to see if she had any text messages. There was one from her friend Jana. They met several months ago after Mercedes came to Bluffton to spend the summer at a cottage and work. They became close friends after Jana contacted Mercedes, asking for help. In a strange turn of events, she and her boyfriend Declan were the means for saving Mercedes' life.

Jana's message was a brief way of checking in to see what Mercedes thought about her new client and that she was praying for Mercedes to have an uneventful job experience for a change. Then she said something that made Mercedes wince.

Declan told me that Zach was approached by an independent filmmaker about making a movie covering his role with taking down Roland and his father. He learned you were not consulted, and he said no. But he told Declan if anyone contacts you and you want to write a book about it, he was willing to help.

It was still difficult for Mercedes to think about her former boyfriend, Zach. When her summer began, they were a couple, though not committed. He was her substitute for Quincy for about a year after Quincy turned down her ultimatum about their future. Afterwards, an old vendetta against her family that she had never heard of became a dangerous showdown, and Zach declared she had ruined his life. He left Hilton Head without even checking on her when men tried to murder her.

Later, Zach showed up at her job at Majestic Oaks Plantation to stop Roland from killing her, ready to die if necessary to end the vendetta once he learned the link he had to Roland.

She sighed, wondering how to respond to Jana's message, then texted back. *I just arrived at Seashell Cottage. You know how much I appreciate your prayers! Let's get together soon. As for Zach, tell Declan I said that I hope he is still healing well and that the law practice is satisfying. I'm glad he won't make a movie about what happened, as if any film maker could re-create that evening! I have no plans to write a book.*

Mercedes finished checking her email and texts on her cell phone and flipped open the woven straw flap of a small crossbody purse she would wear to go into the house. The phone slid into a silky inside pocket, and she snapped the flap down again, ready to gather the things she needed for the job and step out of the Jeep to look around.

Expect the unexpected from an unseen enemy.

Mercedes gasped and her work tablet slipped from her hands. Sitting straight up in the seat, she blinked and looked around. But she was alone, and after collecting herself, she drew a shaky breath.

Those words, recalled from her Great-Great Grand Aunt's old journal and quoted to her by her grandfather recently, had just popped into her mind. Her senses were tingling, but she saw nothing in the lazy summer setting around her to be alert for.

With a long sigh, Mercedes closed her eyes and relaxed back against the headrest in her seat. Taking a few days off before this job would have been a good idea. To describe the past week as being unnerving was an understatement, but asking for a delay with a job meant an inconvenience for her clients.

An image flashed in her mind of a custom-made silver clasp on the black medical bag her brother inherited. It was engraved with crossed swords in a background representing light and dark, evil and holiness, and a reminder from a friend to her ancestor that a Christian's battle is not against flesh and blood.

Opening her eyes, she whispered with conviction, "Expect the unexpected from an unseen enemy."

A tap on her window made her jump. With a nervous laugh at herself, she gestured to a young lady that she was opening the door. She gathered her things again and opened the door to get out.

"I'm so sorry I scared you!" Traces of the Lowcountry danced through the young lady's slow accent and she absently flipped up the ends of her sleek light brown hair from her shoulders. "You're Mercedes Ellison, right? I'm Lacey Ladson. I just arrived in town. Being late is my worst habit, but I am working on moving past it. Among the other things I'm leaving behind."

Mercedes caught the pain in Lacey's soft brown eyes at her last statement. She half expected to see the glitter from a tear in those thick, fringy lashes.

"No problem, Lacey. I was early and then I suddenly remembered something while I was getting my work tablet. In the distraction, I didn't hear your car drive up."

They smiled at one another, and Lacey's dimples were charming. Mercedes knew she was going to like her new client.

Lacey said, "Well, come on, then. I'll check on the yard and gardens before it gets hot, since I told the caretaker she could have the morning off. She wants me to be sure there is still water in the bird bath. The birds really depend on it in temperatures like we've been having."

She turned to the front yard with a gesturing arm to follow her. "I don't know if the grounds of my grandma's house are needed for your paperwork. Mama didn't tell me what you'd be looking for. Do you mind wandering around out here a bit? I promise not to keep you long."

"Oh, of course not! I'm delighted, and if the grounds have any historical elements to them, I can use that in my report."

"Then I must tell you that the brickwork on that walkway over there is salvaged from a well that was here in the 1800s, before the house was built. And let me show you the old summer house out back," Lacey said as they checked a magnificent, sculpted shell basin bird bath that was weathered to a verdigris patina. Several dripping bluebirds flew up into the branches of an ancient magnolia, watching Lacey as she peered into the bowl.

Satisfied, she turned back to Mercedes and led her down a path of scalloped shell shaped steppingstones. "Of course, in your profession, you know that a summer house is a quaint word for a gazebo. But my grandma called it that, and I've always loved the dreamy sound. Isn't it romantic? Oh, I've spent so many amazing summers in this yard and in this house. It's like a miracle to have gotten the job here in Beaufort! It will be my refuge, a place to start fresh, and bring life back into the place again."

Mercedes caught another fleeting, haunted look in Lacey's eyes, but the young woman turned quickly and pointed out camellia bushes that had been transplanted from historic varieties on a local plantation.

When Lacey Ladson finished giving Mercedes a tour of the enchanting gardens and summer house, she led her to a sprawling screened back porch with comfortable furnishings for relaxing. "We'll do this backwards today, if that's all right," she said brightly as she slipped a key in the lock. "This storm door locks instead of having one of those hook thingies, so we can get inside. Then there's a lock from the porch to the kitchen."

Mercedes snapped photos of the porch with her tablet as her client led her into the house. "My great-great grandparents are the original builders of this house, but my great grandparents remodeled it a lot to bring it up to modern standards. You probably have all that information already, so I'm just prattling on. It's not as old as many other historic homes around here, but it's built on a property that had a building on it before the Civil War. My grandmother, I call her Grandy Anna, had a mysterious divorce no one talked about and returned here with my mom, who was little, and her big brother, to live with my great grands. When Grandy Anna married again, the man I knew as my Grampy—her second husband—came from Florida to live here, though his company was there. Years later, my dad started working for Grampy, and that's how Mama met him."

Looking all around, Mercedes said, "Don't be concerned that you're giving me too much information, Lacey. Often, a house and its contents say a lot about its history for those who know what to look for. But the personal stories help weave things together."

She jotted down notes in her tablet about the high ceilings in the cottage that were so prevalent in Lowcountry buildings. There were plenty of windows, as well, built to catch breezes for ventilation.

Lacey started chatting again as she led Mercedes through the kitchen to a simple but classic back staircase. "Let's start upstairs and come down through the front grand staircase. These stairs are great for coming down to the kitchen and getting to the back porch and yard in the mornings. My grandparents' house has a lot of features few people know about, and I love them all. Oh, my summers and vacations here were wonderful! When I moved off to college and worked out-of-state right afterwards, I missed coming back."

At the top of the stairs, a large window filled the passage with natural light. Diffused daylight spread from another direction over the hallway to the bedrooms. Mercedes looked up and said, "Is the light coming from the cupola on the roof?"

"Yes, it's near the middle of the house, above the grand staircase and entry. Here's the first bedroom, and it has a surprise. Come on in, I'll show you."

Mercedes smiled at Lacey's enthusiasm and stepped into a room that looked like it was out of a Southern decorating magazine. Her first impression was of the unique shell-shaped fan displayed in a clean fireplace grate. "Oh," she breathed, forgetting to take notes about the architecture.

But Lacey's attention was on surprising her guest. In a moment, she opened a section of the built-in bookcases to access the next bedroom. "Grandy called this a Murphy door, and it's always fascinated me! The next room was mine when I stayed here, and this one was Mama and Daddy's. When I was little and got afraid at night, my parents left this open."

Delighted, Mercedes went through the opening to the next room. She said, "I don't see many of these. But then, I'm not supposed to, am I? Jib doors were once popular in European estates, where people had secret lives."

"That's what my Grandy told me," Lacey said. "He also had an ancestor who kept daggers hanging under important portraits in case of a fire, to cut the canvases quickly from the frames and roll them up to be saved. Can you imagine?"

She giggled and added, "I wonder how many times those daggers became a quick threat in an argument."

Mercedes took notes while her client led her through spacious, beautiful old rooms filled with quaint, elegant Lowcountry inspired cottage décor such as magnolia blooms filling fireplace grates and carved palm designs on panels over double doorways. Pale, breezy colors on the walls and airy, lacy drapes gave every room a calm, relaxing feel. Seashell designs were used in the décor of every room.

The top of the grand staircase was glorious in the sunlight that spilled down from the copula above. Mercedes marveled that the owners of a home they humbly called a cottage could create such casual beauty.

As they descended to the entryway, she admired the palm fan shaped carving under an arch and said, "My idea of what I thought I wanted in my home someday has disappeared."

Lacey laughed. "Yes, this house has a way of inspiring people," she said. "There are larger and much more important homes in Beaufort, but none have the style and personality of our cottage."

She led Mercedes through large pots of tropical foliage that flanked the bottom of the stairs and took her into the dining room on the left. Like many old Beaufort homes, the dining and drawing rooms opened to the enormous entry hall for entertaining crowds and were closed with sliding doors for privacy.

Though the dining room furnishings were all graceful and unique, it was the fireplace that stopped Mercedes in her tracks.

Artisans delicately carved the large mantle with a variety of seashells, coral, and graceful seaweed that surrounded the pale coral-pink stone. She took a photo before walking over to peer at the details. "I've seen nothing like this."

"As far as I know, there's not another one. My great-grandparents had it custom made. You see, my great-grandmother loved and collected seashells. Great grandpa asked her to plan the dining room in her own taste, and he decorated the drawing room across the hallway."

Mercedes reluctantly turned from admiring the mantle. "That must be the room with the closed sliding doors in the entry hallway."

"Yes, and it's usually open," Lacey said, walking toward the entry again. "But our caretaker, Margie, cleans the house inside and she probably just dusted the door moldings. You'd be surprised how dusty things get here in town."

Expect the unexpected from an unseen enemy.

Startled at thinking these words again, Mercedes hesitated, then opened her mouth to warn Lacey to wait. In a moment, she changed her mind. She might feel spooked over a closed door, but Lacey was not.

"Old family stories say the roosters came in here after dinner to get away from the hens," Lacey was saying. She giggled and glanced back at her guest while sliding the double doors into the pockets built for them inside the walls. "I suppose in the days before television, men and women gathered with friends for quality time and conversation."

Mercedes came to stand by her client, who had turned back to the drawing room and stood staring. Lacey turned a confused look at her and gulped. Then she stammered, "I've never seen that—that hideous black cabinet before. It doesn't belong here."

Chapter 2

The intruding cabinet dominated the drawing room at Seashell Cottage. The soft hair on Mercedes's neck felt like it stood against the collar of her new blouse.

"I've seen nothing like it," Lacey said in a tight, hushed tone. She stood rooted in the doorway as if repelled by some force emitting from the black lacquered wood.

"No one would have," Mercedes said, almost under her breath. "This is a custom piece made for a very particular person or purpose, Lacey." She clinched her fist and fought against the urge to fly out the front door.

Lacey reached out for Mercedes' arm. "Don't touch it," she whispered. "Something might happen."

She looked into Lacey's eyes, which were filled with fear and pleading, and nodded. "Don't worry, this is already closer than I want to be to that thing. Why do you think something might happen if we touch it? Are you frightened only because it doesn't belong here?"

With a shiver, Lacey rubbed her arms with her hands and turned to look at the cabinet. "Maybe. I honestly can't explain what is happening to me, and I don't know why I said not to touch it. That was silly, wasn't it?"

Lacey looked sheepishly at Mercedes and said, "For some reason, I feel a sense of dread. And I want this hideous monstrosity out of here!" Then her voice squeaked. "See those wicked claws? And is the weird long thing a Sphinx?"

Mercedes followed her eyes. "Yes, the cabinet has feet of carved talons. It's decorated with Egyptian religious symbols."

And they represent gods of death and the afterlife, she thought. But she kept what she knew about the symbols on the cabinet to herself. Instead, she said, "My fiancé and his father are both archaeologists and antiquities experts. They could tell us what this is, if they were here."

Lacey pursed her lips and scowled at the designs. "Look, I don't want to insult other people's ideas. They can believe what they want. But this thing creeps me out."

Mercedes smiled grimly at Lacey's response. There was no reason to share that the Sphinx was thought to be far older than the Egyptian dynasty represented on the rest of the cabinet, and the head had been changed at least once. There was no record of what hybrid animal or human head was original and what god it was intended to honor. And the symbols and hieroglyphics that unnerved them both? No reason to share her certainty that this cabinet was profoundly linked to death.

And worse, there was no reason to tell Lacey the only possible explanation for it being here was that it was a message.

Lacey Ladson had lost her enthusiasm for showing off her grandmother's beloved house. She was distracted, struggling to recover her poise as she led Mercedes around. As in the dining room, there was another custom-made mantle in this one, carved with nautical themes, and another Murphy door in a bookcase that led to a bathroom and the back staircase. Over the mantle was a large painting of a group of sailboats.

Lacey pointed to the painting. "My grandfather had a sailboat, and one of these looks like it. He and his sailing friends used to come in here to tell old stories and relive their memories."

Then she turned to several items of furniture that were out of place. "These are usually against the wall where that cabinet is."

She sighed and stopped. "I'm sorry, Mercedes, but do you mind if I call my mama? You can look around to see the rest of the first floor if you like. My grandparent's master bedroom is down the hallway."

"Of course," Mercedes said. "Listen—if it makes you feel any better, I understand your discomfort. The cabinet—it disturbs me, too."

Relief filled Lacey's soft brown eyes, and she laid her hand on Mercedes' arm. "Then you don't think I'm silly, and you know I can't sleep in this house tonight until I find out what has happened."

Mercedes held the young woman's eyes. "I do. And if you don't find out, don't stay here alone. Never doubt your instincts when something doesn't feel right, Lacey."

Seashell Cottage would not be the easy in-and-out job Mercedes had longed for. Maybe she was a curse and should give up on her career as an independent Architectural Historian. She always seemed to arrive when her clients' lives were upended.

These were the foremost thoughts in her mind as she squeezed her eyes shut and leaned against the doorframe of the main bedroom. But her growing unease made her open them again. *Be sober-minded and alert*, she thought, remembering 1

Peter 5:8 from her Bible. *Your adversary, the devil, is prowling about like a roaring lion, looking for anyone he can devour.*

Unless her imagination ran wild, a spiritual adversary was prowling, all right.

Her heart raced. If only she could settle down and go through her routine to get what she needed, she could finish her part in this job and turn in the report to the Ladson family. The black cabinet had nothing to do with her, and they could solve the situation on their own.

She drew a deep, ragged breath to slow the adrenaline rush surging inside her. It was time to get back to work. Stepping into the room, she touched the screen on her tablet and recorded what she needed before moving on.

Lacey's voice had been distant and indistinct, but then she walked up to Mercedes in the hallway and handed over her cell phone. "My mother asked if she could speak to you. Do you mind?"

Seeing Lacey's fear made a well of calm courage rise in Mercedes. She nodded and put the phone up to her ear while walking into the kitchen. "This is Mercedes Ellison," she said.

"Mercedes, Annette Ladson here," said her client. "We've been emailing, but we spoke on the phone a month or so ago when we were trying to arrange our schedules to get paperwork completed on the cottage."

"Of course. It's pleasant to speak with you again, Annette. Is there anything I can do while I'm here with your daughter?"

Annette Ladson sighed. When she spoke again, she did not hide her stress. "Mercedes, I'm going to travel up there from Florida, but I won't arrive until after midnight in the early morning. There are no other keys to the cottage than what the caretaker, me, and Lacey have, and yet someone has made an unwanted furniture delivery without our permission. Lacey was planning to move in today, but now, that isn't possible. Her safety is at stake."

She hesitated, and Mercedes braced herself. Should she offer to help Lacey?

"This is asking a lot," Annette began, "but, if you have no other appointments, is it possible for you to join my daughter in town for shopping and lunch until I call with an arrangement for her?"

"Oh. Yes, of course, Annette. I'll be glad to help. I was planning to shop and sightsee here this afternoon, anyway. Are you calling law enforcement? This is serious. You should change the locks right away."

"I have a close friend from high school who still lives nearby, and he's a private detective. I'll call him first and I'll see what he recommends."

Mercedes looked over at Lacey, who watched wide-eyed with her fingers on her lips to keep them from trembling. "I understand. Lacey and I will leave the house right now and stay in public places until you contact her with the next step we should take. Is there anything I should know about this situation?"

"Before Lacey called me, I wouldn't have thought so. Now I wonder. I'm just confused, but I'll talk to Cowboy and see what he thinks."

Mercedes blinked and her brows shot up. "Cowboy?" she asked.

"That's my friend's nickname. He grew up raising horses and wore boots and a hat. His manner is relaxed and disarming, but make no mistake, Mercedes, he's as sharp as they come, and he has insights, law enforcement experience, and unusual connections that few others do."

Lacey and Mercedes left the house the way they had come in, locking up the back doors and walking into the mood-lifting sunshine of the warm late summer day. The shaded areas had moved with the angle of the sun, and the landscape had taken on a different look. Birds played in the fresh water in the birdbath, but they flapped glistening droplets from their wet wings in the sunlight rather than the shade.

As the two young ladies strolled toward their cars in the front driveway, Lacey chatted about the foods she was excited to have again in the local restaurants. A shadow in Mercedes' peripheral vision caught her attention, and she quickly turned to see a figure jerk back from a small open spot on the outside sidewalk side of the tall privacy hedge in front of the property.

Her heart jumped. She kept walking, since they were moving that way, and she raised her hand over her eyes and squinted to note any details. But whoever had been watching the house was now gone, and she had no way of knowing which direction they had taken.

"What do you think?" she heard Lacey ask.

Mercedes blinked and turned to her. Lacey repeated her question, adding, "About where to eat for lunch."

"Which one has the best salad?" Mercedes asked. "I'm in the mood for something cool and crisp for lunch."

Lacey brightened and smiled. They had reached the driveway, and she made her way to her car door to open it. "Well, then, just follow my car," she said. "I've got you!"

Mercedes returned the smile, then peered again at the hedge before going around to get into her Jeep. But there was no sign of anyone.

As she started the engine and snapped her seat belt, she decided not to tell Lacey about the incident. But she made a note of what time it was, in case it was something she should report to anyone later.

Why was someone secretly watching the house?

Lacey and Mercedes enjoyed a pleasant lunch in town, but their conversation was awkward. The sudden, uneasy situation that had forced their schedules into an afternoon together was unlike an outing with old friends. Lacey was surprised when Mercedes offered to give thanks for their meal after the server put it on the table. She put her fork back down and bowed her head. When she opened her eyes, she looked around to see if anyone had noticed.

Mercedes almost smiled at Lacey's embarrassment. Her young client was raised in church, she knew, from conversations with her mother. But Mercedes well remembered the peer reactions to her own expressions of faith, even in Christian private schools. Students who felt the need to say a prayer learned that it was easier to say a silent one. Yet, the bold students were the ones who rose as leaders. She learned from their example to live out her faith in confidence.

But Mercedes looked around the restaurant for another reason. Her family taught her to make a habit of checking her surroundings when she was in an unfamiliar or public place. In a nearby corner, a young, reddish-blonde man wearing the uniform of the Lowcountry—resort casual attire—was trying to hide his interest in them. Though he sat alone, when not glancing at them, he focused on eating his sub sandwich and French fries as politely as possible for such a hand-held meal. He sat up straight and chewed bites of food well, looking at the view out the window to the foot traffic in the street, not on a cell phone. Mercedes gave him a five-star rating for good table manners and the ability to observe the world around him.

Turning her attention back to her own meal and manners, she said, "So, Lacey, tell me more about the new job you have here in Beaufort. When is your first day?"

She smiled across the small table, where Lacey stared with unseeing eyes out the window, chewing a bite of her deli sandwich. "Oh," Lacey replied, looking back at her new friend and returning her smile with a quick, small quirk of her lips. "I'll be a property manager for several gated communities. This is such a lovely area to be involved in properties, you know. I'm starting on Monday."

"It's easy to see why you're excited about it. Does your family still have friends around here?" Mercedes asked.

Lacey swallowed another bite of her sandwich and sipped some iced sweet tea before answering. "My Mama has friends from church and school who are still in town," she replied. "But I was a teenager the last time I went to church here, and I'm not sure anyone I met is still around."

"Will you be going there this Sunday?" Mercedes ventured. "I can't think of a better place than a familiar church for meeting new friends. And maybe even someone who will become more than just a friend."

Lacey grimaced before waving a hand in the air to dismiss those ideas. "I don't go to church anymore."

Mercedes set down her fork and dabbed her mouth with her napkin, praying for discernment and the right words to carry on with this conversation. But Lacey changed the subject quicker than she could end her prayer.

"I was supposed to marry someone, you know, instead of coming here," her young client blurted out. "But after technical college and going to real estate training, I came back to find out he was days away from a wedding to someone else. No wonder he never gave me an engagement ring or let me announce an engagement. Friends told me he's been stringing me along for over a year while being engaged to her. And she's the one who had a ring."

Open-mouthed, Mercedes watched Lacey's eyes redden. They swam in unshed tears. She reached into her purse and stretched her hand across the table with a small pack of tissues.

"Oh, Lacey, I don't know what to say," she almost whispered. "I meant to encourage you about meeting a special guy, not to bring up painful memories."

A movement in the corner where the man was watching made her glance his way, and she caught him watching them again. He met her eyes and glanced down, picking up the small black folder the server had left on his table with his bill.

Lacey accepted the tissues, dabbing her eyes and blowing her nose. She sniffed and drew a deep breath. Soon, she was back in control. "Thank you," she managed in a raspy voice. She cleared her throat and slid the tissue pack back across the tablecloth to Mercedes. "It's not your fault at all; it's just been a strange day. I'm a bundle of jumping nerves."

She sighed, then looked down at herself and smiled. "The woman he married was slender. That's not how anyone would describe me, so I guess his preferences changed. But he could have been honest—with both of us."

Two things happened at once before Mercedes could reply. Lacey's mobile phone rang, and the server came to the table to clear away dishes and ask if the check was together or separate.

"Together, please," Mercedes said while Lacey pulled her phone from her bag and answered the call. Lacey greeted her mother and met Mercedes' eyes.

Mercedes overheard Annette was going to text Cowboy's phone number to both Lacey and Mercedes. The server returned, and she slid the cash into the folder, telling him to keep the change, while she heard Lacey protest about something her mother said.

Annette asked to speak with Mercedes again, so she took the phone offered to her. "Hi, Mrs. Ladson, this is Mercedes."

Her client's voice was tense and weary as she said, "Mercedes, it's fine to call me Annette. I've discussed the situation at the cottage with Cowboy, and he will investigate for me in the morning. He says no police yet. But I have a problem. Like me, he thinks it's too risky for Lacey to stay alone there tonight, or even in a hotel, since we don't know if she's being followed. It appears that someone knew she would be arriving. We're uncertain how anyone received that information."

Mercedes instinctively looked up to see if the young man in the corner was still watching. But he was heading into the small hallway to the men's restroom.

No, she thought. *He was just curious about me and Lacey. Right?*

Annette's voice broke through her speculation when she said, "Cowboy could put her up in one of his guest rooms, but he's a Christian, so he shouldn't have a single woman there alone overnight. It matters with appearances in the community, where he is well known. As a Christian yourself, you see my dilemma. I know you are allergic to indoor pets, and he assured me the only animals he has are his perpetual few cows and horses, which are outdoors. He has no time left for cleaning up after a dog or cat."

Mercedes' mind was reeling at this turn of events. Annette was right to be concerned about protecting Lacey at this point, and in her mind, she saw the black cabinet. Mercedes' gut instinct told her it was a threat, a warning.

Before she had time to think, she found herself saying, "Oh. Yes, I do see. Well, I have no plans tonight. If it will ease your mind, I can spend the afternoon with Lacey and then we'll meet up with your friend when he's ready."

Relief filled Annette's voice, and she rushed to say, "Oh, Mercedes, would you? Of course, I will pay for your time and for any personal items you need to pick up to spend the night and wear tomorrow. From your website and our conversations, I feel like I can trust you, and for a reason I can't get into over the phone, I'm sure the Lord has put you here to help me. I don't mean to sound mysterious, Mercedes, but no one else could be better to have here with us right now. I'll explain it tomorrow at the cottage. It will help Lacey if you and Cowboy are there."

"For all that this is a weird situation, I admit I'm having fun," Lacey said, shifting her shopping tote bag up her arm as she rummaged through colorful flip flops and selecting a pink pair with bold daisy blooms on them. She and Mercedes had been ducking into local boutiques and gift shops ever since leaving the restaurant, seeking the air conditioning and browsing the shelves.

Mercedes needed something to sleep in for her unexpected overnight stay. She smiled at Lacey and replied, "Yes, I was going to shop here this afternoon, anyway. I just didn't expect to pick up something to wear tomorrow. And a tee shirt and loose shorts to sleep in. What do you think of this one?"

In her hands was a white tee shirt with two cruiser bicycles on a boardwalk, as if waiting for their riders to finish a sunset walk on the beach. Under the picture was the longitude and latitude for Beaufort, South Carolina.

"You're sure you don't want the one with the kissing flamingos with cocktails?" Lacey said, then her face crumpled into laughter.

With a grin, Mercedes replied, "I don't drink, and though I love flamingos, that neon pink cartoon style is not for me. Besides, my fiancé would hate it."

"What's he like?" Lacey asked, turning her back to try on a pair of sunglasses. "Will he be upset that you aren't coming home tonight?"

Mercedes hesitated, realizing that Lacey thought she lived with Quincy. She said, "He's a consultant for antiquities, archaeology, and history. His name is Quincy, and I'll text him in a little while to update him about my change in plans. Right now, he's finishing a contract for a dig site in St. Augustine, then he'll come back to Bluffton. Each of us rented a cottage there for the summer. He stays down the street from me."

She knew Lacey was studying her in the little tilted mirror on the sunglasses rack. Then she turned and slid a pair up to her face. "What do you think of this style?" she asked. "I need some new ones to carry in my purse."

"They're flattering, and that's a good deal with the sale price. Do you need a case to protect them in your bag?"

"Oh, yes, I should get one. My car was too small to pack many clothes and accessories, plus my computer. Both of us are kind of getting by with some basics tonight, aren't we?"

"Which reminds me we need to run to a grocery store," Mercedes said. "I'm going to need a toothbrush and toothpaste, and maybe a few food items just in case."

Lacey's phone chimed with a text notification, so Mercedes took her purchases from her arm to free her to check the message. "Cowboy just introduced himself and sent me his address," she said, squinting at the phone screen. "He says he'll be home after four o'clock, just to text him when we know what time to expect us."

"That gives us time to check out, get to our cars, and run to the grocery store," Mercedes said. "Ask him if he needs anything from the store for dinner."

Lacey keyed in the message and got a quick reply. She looked up with a grin and answered. "He said he raises his own cows for grass-fed steaks, and he picked up russet potatoes, carrots, green beans, and strawberries at his neighbor's vegetable stand today."

"Your mom's old friend gets more interesting every time we talk about him," Mercedes said with a wry smile. She said a silent prayer of thanks for this brighter look in the evening's uncertainty ahead.

Chapter 3

Cowboy's house was at the end of a long road lined with forest and pastures. Lazy cattle moved closer to a white barn, and horses raised their heads behind white fences, curious about Lacey and Mercedes' cars coming onto the property.

As the long ranch-style house came into view, a large body of water sparkled behind it. Mercedes followed Lacey's compact car to a driveway in front of a three-car garage, where they parked and gathered their things for the night. A lanky, suntanned man wearing a western hat came out of the house to greet them.

"You must be Cowboy," Lacey said, and he laughed. It was a deep, genuine laugh, from a grounded soul, and without knowing the man yet, Mercedes was sure it suited him.

"What gave me away?" he replied, winking and tipping his hat respectfully. "I'm Chris Coulter, but everyone calls me Cowboy. And I believe you're Miss Lacey Ladson. You favor your mother, and that's a compliment."

While Lacey beamed, he turned to Mercedes, who walked up to join them. After a frank, appraising look with his earthy hazel eyes, he gave her a nod and a lazy smile. "No question who you are, Miss Mercedes Ellison," he told her. "You look just like your photos on your website. I'm sure glad to meet you."

"Likewise," Mercedes said, smiling and liking this man instantly. "If you'll just call me Mercedes, I'll call you Cowboy instead of Mr. Cowboy."

With another laugh, he nodded. In his warm voice, he replied, "You're smart and you've got a sense of humor. Leave your bag here and come with us. I'll be back out for it after I get you two settled in the house."

"Wow," Lacey said, beaming as she slid her chair back from the country style wooden table to give her stomach more room. "Everything was so good! I'm stuffed. Can I wait a bit to have the strawberries and whipped coconut cream?"

"Yes, this was a fabulous dinner," Mercedes agreed, setting her water glass down by her plate, which was now empty of the hearty, yet simple, meal that Cowboy had cooked for them. "I need to wait for dessert, too. Perhaps we can enjoy it on the deck overlooking the water before the sun sets?"

Cowboy grinned. "Looks like I won't need to change my habits tonight," he said. "I usually wind down with dessert out there at the end of the day."

Lacey's cell phone vibrated again in her pocket, as it had several times during dinner, and Mercedes was glad hers would not be an interruption. She had already texted Quincy to tell him of her change in plans and her landlord to say not to watch for her to be home.

Lacey sighed and said, "I have so-o-o-o many texts to answer. Do you mind if I go to my room for a little while to let friends know I'm okay, but not at the house yet? I'll join you again later for those strawberries and the view."

"Of course," Cowboy replied. "But Lacey, don't say anything about the real reason you're here tonight. It's too soon to tell anyone about the cabinet, and after tomorrow, you may not want them to know at all. You'll still be honest if you tell them your mother needs to check on something the caretaker didn't know about."

Lacey considered her host's advice, then said, "You're right. If I bring it up, it will spark a lot of imagination and I'll be on the phone for a long time. The truth is—"

Her eyes darted to the window as she hesitated. After a few moments, she looked at Cowboy, and in a conspiratorial voice, said, "The truth is, I don't want to even think about that scary cabinet. And what would I say? It doesn't belong in my grandparent's house, and it has really upset my mother."

A sad half-smile spread across Cowboy's tanned face. His eyes were as gentle as his voice when he said, "Okay, then go on and catch up with your friends. You'll feel better."

As Lacey left the room, Mercedes said, "After all you've done for us, please let me help with the dishes."

His warm laugh came easily, crinkling the fine lines at the corners of his tanned face as he shook his head. "No, ma'am, I'll load these in the dishwasher. But I would like to talk to you about something after that. Can I show you some books I have in the den?"

Cowboy's den was much like him, as was the rest of his sprawling ranch house. A small open candle tin diffused a faint woodsy scent that worked well with the smell of leather on furniture and books. Large windows provided a stage to observe livestock in the fenced pastures, and two walls of sturdy built-in cabinets housed books and treasured collections of a Southern outdoor sportsman. She assumed one set of closed upper doors hid a television screen until Cowboy wanted it, but she did not see him as a guy who wasted time watching other people's drama or keeping up with football.

Settling into the embrace of a large leather chair, she opened the first book on a small stack of several that her host arranged for her on a side table. Warm light for reading bathed the books and added a glow to a carved wooden sculpture of a man casting a net from a fishing boat.

Mercedes had seen these books in her grandfather's library back home in Charleston, but she avoided them. The titles and topics signaled to her that reading them would demand a response that she was unprepared for. Since Cowboy asked her to glance through them, she felt the topics were sure to relate to the situation at Seashell Cottage.

She was saying a silent prayer for an open heart, open mind, discernment, and a teachable spirit when Cowboy came into the den. He settled into the matching chair on the other side of the small table.

"I read the news about what happened at Majestic Oaks," he said. "What an incredible discovery you made there on the Freedom Staircase! It made me wonder, how much history about the Revolutionary War did you know when you started?"

Mercedes swallowed and looked away from him to the windows and the view of the pastures. "I knew the usual names, locations, and dates that most schools teach about American History. I was often home educated when we were traveling to help on archaeology dig sites with my fiancé's family, and the history curriculum focused on God's work in history. The same was true in private Christian schools I attended. But I was most interested in the men who represented my area in South Carolina, the ones whose names are on many roads, places, and institutions. I'm intrigued by their courage, and their willingness to lose everything and become traitors for a cause they believed in."

She turned to look at him. "I realize it was the unknown, everyday people whose sacrifice and courage won the war. Men such as the ones who risked stopping at Majestic Oaks for messages, shelter, and supplies. The famous people were the leaders who inspired them."

Cowboy nodded and sighed. Unlike most people she met, he was in no rush to plunge into conversation. When he spoke again, he said, "Many of the leaders used a different dictionary than the unnamed, everyday people. They spoke and wrote the same words but had different belief systems and definitions. They intended to be deceptive. For example, the Christian citizens understood the name 'God' from a biblical viewpoint that encompasses Jesus Christ. The Founders that were high level Freemasons had a different vocabulary and a different god. The ones who get invited to rise from the bottom levels know him by other names, such as Lucifer, and he supposedly gives secret knowledge to privileged members."

Mercedes nodded. "And they wanted freedom to practice that religion, which was persecuted in Europe."

Cowboy stretched out his long legs and crossed one leather boot over another as he settled back further into his chair. "True, but their goals were much more complex," he said in his slow drawl. "In every settlement for ages, masons have set up a town square with legal and symbolic establishments to claim territory under their subjection. Ancient peoples knew the land that became America, and some believe it was preserved for this historical era—what Bible scholars call the last days, beginning with Jesus' victory over death.

He seemed lost in thought as he sat staring at his fingertips as he touched them together. "Sir Frances Bacon, the Lord Chancellor of England under King James 1, had a theory that the Americas were where ancient Atlantis could be. He wanted North America to be a grand Masonic experiment, a place to bring back the old gods of enlightenment. He called it the hearth of the New World Order, and his writings about it, called *New Atlantis,* became published after his death."

Then Cowboy turned to meet her eyes. "So, you see, Mercedes, there's no secret about any of it, no conspiracy theories. Secular scholars and historical documents state the purpose of the pagan layout and symbols our capitol rests on, even down to the latitude. The buildings, the monuments, the art, the streets, the names of things, are all significant. Once you see it, you can't unsee it. Accurate history about who is ruling the world differs greatly from what's taught in America's school systems."

The soft leather chair whispered and molded around Mercedes as she sat back in it, closing her eyes. "Oh, yes, I know. When I was working at Majestic Oaks Plantation, I wanted to share the noble view of America's birth with my fiancé, who is American born to an American mother. His father's family is British, and he spent most of his life there in his family's peerage society or around the world in archaeology dig sites. I hoped to show him the close-up struggle for freedom that America won, the foundation for dreams of hard-working people who wanted to build a country where those dreams could come true."

She reached up and rubbed her forehead, pushing aside her blond bangs. Then she turned to look at Cowboy. "He enjoyed learning about American History by seeing how it was lived on Majestic Oaks. But afterwards, he suggested that someday we should go to Washington, DC. When I thought about what I could show him there, I went cold. I'm glad we once appreciated beauty in architecture, which no longer exists in public buildings. But everywhere Quincy would look, through the eyes of his profession, there are pagan temples and references to pagan deities."

Cowboy studied her face and sighed, nodding his head in sympathy. "If America was founded as a Christian nation, our nation's capital would have crosses, references to Jesus, and other Biblical monuments. It would have been appropriate for Christians to give the glory to Jesus Christ for their improbable and miraculous establishment as a nation where they are free to worship him."

With a wave of her hand, Mercedes grasped for the right words to tell her host something that had been on her heart. "If Quincy went to DC, he'd feel like he was walking through a pagan Roman or Greek city. He'd recognize Freemason symbols everywhere. He already commented on what the Washington Monument's obelisk symbolizes in Egyptian history, and how the Capitol building dome goes with it. There's nothing remotely Christian about them."

"Quincy knows the monuments and buildings have a spiritual charge and are territorial," Cowboy replied. "Unseen rituals are being held in honor of the occult deities represented everywhere. When you see pictures online of the Washington Monument and the Statue of Liberty being struck by lightning, don't assume it came from God as a warning. It's likely to be ritual activity."

Mercedes squirmed in the soft chair again, processing his words while looking back out the window. The late day serenity of the pastureland soothed her tension about this topic.

"You've had a busy summer, if the local news is to be believed," Cowboy said. His voice was low, calm, and straightforward. "Have you had time to come to any conclusions about the things you're mulling over?"

She blinked and sighed before turning to him to reply. "I don't want to admit that I have, but I'm going to say this out loud for the first time. When the world turned upside down in 2020, I frantically prayed that Jesus would help me understand how America had completely abandoned the vision of its founders. You see, I was looking at it from my Christian definition of those principles. I knew that secret societies kept the ages-long tradition of setting up, shaping, and controlling countries behind the scenes, but I assumed even the Freemason founders operated with a Judeo-Christian foundation. That was wrong. And every day, Jesus brought startling, unsettling information into my life, from unexpected sources I never would have sought. One day, I realized He had answered my prayer for understanding. It was an eye-opening moment. Honestly, it was a shock."

Mercedes hesitated. Her hand flew up to her mouth. Her eyes met Cowboy's earthy hazel ones before she put her hand on her lap and spoke. "The truth is, my country here on earth isn't a Christian nation, as I was taught, and the true vision of the Freemasons and other secret societies among the Founders is being fulfilled. The goal has always been to become a New World Order. Now, my prayer is that Jesus' will be done on earth as it is in heaven, whether he steps in to stop this, or he brings in the harvest of his people."

Cowboy nodded with approval. "I'm relieved to hear that the Lord answered your prayer for understanding, even though it was painful."

"For most of my life," she said, "I've overlooked how significant the things I knew, and things I saw, were, because I believed patriotic songs and sentiments. That's the country I wanted in an imperfect world. Many of the pieces of the puzzle were in my mind, from other studies and biographies, but I wasn't ready to put them together. Little did I know how the picture would look when the Lord gave me the grace and vision to see it. It astounds me how few people see."

With a gentle tone, Cowboy said, "Freemasonry was successful and influential in colonizing America. But some Colonial Freemasons thought they served the God of the Bible, which Ben Franklin disliked. Satan cloaks much of it in a type of Christianity, because perverting the truth is what he does. It's all he has. He's a god with no light to give and no secret knowledge higher than Jesus gives us. Even today, the lower levels don't know what they are involved in, but they do know that they honor and serve a system built on lies and deception. It is wrong when Christians swear death oaths and take part in occult rituals to other gods and that they are colluding with each other for the 'leg up' over their fellow man. They join for the privileges of the network."

Mercedes grimaced and nodded. "Yes. I recently read a quote by John Quincy Adams in which he said Freemasonry is a seed of evil that can't produce any good," she said. "He believed that it was the greatest, or at least one of the greatest moral and political evils our country was struggling with. From the evidence, I believe this is still true. Secret societies set themselves above others, creating a privileged class for themselves, and this naturally builds a distain for outsiders. But Christianity, in contrast, is where mankind cannot save themselves with good deeds and all are equal in the eyes of Jesus, who is the Light of the World. There are no secrets – the Gospel and sound doctrine are to be shared openly with everyone. I like the way John Quincy Adams put it—Freemasonry is a conspiracy of the few against equal rights of the many. He said it should be abolished forever."

"It's about blood, Mercedes," Cowboy said. But Lacey's voice cut him short as she stepped into the library.

"There you are!" she said. "I finished letting my friends know I'm all right, and I can't get those beautiful strawberries off my mind. What time is dessert?"

"Right now," drawled Cowboy, winking at Mercedes and rising slowly from his chair. "Let's grab our plates and go out to the porch. The sun is about to put on a show as it goes to light up the other side of the world."

After Mercedes settled into a comfortable guest bed for the night, she yawned and set her alarm on her cellphone. Then she opened a text to send to Quincy.

She typed a few words, then erased those and tried again. After a weary sigh and erasing her words once more, she sent a message. *There's so much I want to talk to you about, Quincy, but I'm simply too tired to think straight right now. I'm safely tucked in at my client's friend's home. Can we catch up tomorrow? Is everything okay there with you?*

In a few moments, a text message from Quincy interrupted her random, drowsy prayers. *Things are about the same here. But it will be over in a couple of days. I'm tired and discouraged, and now I'm concerned about you and your situation. I checked into the friend of your client, and that gives me peace of mind about tonight. But I'm uneasy about what you're walking into tomorrow.*

Mercedes wanted Quincy to relax and get the rest he badly needed. She sat up against her pillow to think more clearly about her message, then typed it. *Something popped into my head several times this morning. My grandfather said this to me recently, and it was in my great grand aunt's journal. The words were, "Expect the unexpected from an unseen enemy." In the morning, check your phone when you get a break. I will send photos of a black lacquered cabinet that was brought into my client's home under mysterious circumstances. I promise you will be intrigued by the Egyptian designs on it, representing death and the afterlife. Please, try to relax and sleep tonight. Pray for me to be ready for whatever I encounter, and I'll be praying for you.*

Soon, Quincy texted back. *I wish I could see the cabinet in person. My dad once dealt with a case of three identical black cabinets like that. Stay alert and take those strange words in your mind seriously. I will be praying for you and loving you always.*

Chapter 4

"No, no. I want it destroyed. If you can't do it, just say so. I have options."

Mercedes awakened to Cowboy's deep voice somewhere outside, and his tone made her brows raise. She glanced at the small clock on the bedside table.

"It's not for sale, but I'll pay for your work. Call me back if you're interested," she heard her host say. Lack of another voice meant he must be on a phone call, and she sat up, looking at her window. It faced the beautiful view of the pier from a long, covered porch where they had enjoyed dessert last night.

She resisted going to the window to listen for his voice to rise again. The only sound was the thud of a door, and she mulled over what she had heard and what it may mean.

With her eyes closed again, she prayed about facing a day with no idea what it would bring. Her heart filled with praises and that the Lord's will be done on earth as it is in heaven, and she asked Jesus for wisdom, discernment, and safety for everyone involved in the situation at Seashell Cottage. Then she prayed that he would reveal what should be known about the mysterious appearance of the unwelcome, ominous black cabinet. "Please remove any place where evil can hide and bring it out to face the light of your truth and justice," she whispered. "If it brings you glory, weave all that was meant for harm to come to good, for your purpose and your time under heaven. Amen."

Mercedes checked her phone for a weather forecast and top news headlines. Then she gathered what she needed for a shower. The hallway and Lacey's room were silent, but the enticing smells of breakfast made her guess Cowboy was enjoying his.

As she dressed for the day ahead, her mind puzzled over whether her host planned to pay someone to destroy the Egyptian black cabinet rather than making a profit from a sale. It would be worth money, and a lot of it, in certain circles, but she, too, would rather see it be destroyed.

The homey scents of food wafted through the house and teased her growling stomach. Glancing over at her phone charging on the nightstand, Mercedes noticed she had a text. She reached to get her charger and the phone for her purse and smiled when she saw it was from Quincy. Her fiancé wished her a good day and asked for a date to talk sometime around lunchtime.

It still felt strange to think of Quincy this way. "My fiancé," she whispered, musing that they had finally reached this status. If only no hurdles remained for them to cross.

Her response to his message wished him a great day ahead, said that she missed him, and she would let him know if she could call. With a satisfied glance around the guest room, she left it as neatly as she had found it last night.

In the hallway, a sleepy-eyed, tousled Lacey almost bumped into her on her way to the bathroom. The younger girl giggled, mumbled a good morning, and waved a lavender paisley toiletry bag at the bathroom door.

"I have some maintenance work to do before anyone can see me today," she announced with a grin. "But I'm starving! Save me some of whatever smell is so divine!"

Mercedes was still smiling at her encounter with Lacey as she made her way toward the kitchen and sat her tote bag and purse down in the hallway. A man's voice teaching a Christian Bible Study was coming through the doorway.

At the stove, a woman with graying hair and a beaming smile turned to see her come in. Mercedes wished her a good morning, and the woman turned, wiping her hands in a field of daisies across the front of her clean apron.

"Yes, it surely is a good mornin'. I'm Louisa, Cowboy's part-time housekeeper," she announced, extending her hand.

"I'm Mercedes. Thank you so much for making breakfast," Mercedes said, squeezing Louisa's hand and smiling.

Louisa kept her hand and studied her. She said, "You have an unusual name, and you're not what I imagined."

Mercedes laughed at the housekeeper's straightforward observation. She was accustomed to people being surprised when they met her. "You expected a sultry, dark-haired beauty, I think. But I ended up with the blonde genes in the family, and no, I wasn't born in the back seat of a luxury car. I'm named after a Great-Grand Aunt, and yes, she had Spanish heritage somewhere back in her ancestry."

Louisa released her hand and chuckled. "That's a clever idea, being named after a car you may have been born in." She waved toward the table. "Come on in for some breakfast. Cowboy left me a menu for you and Lacey."

She poured a cup of herbal tea as Mercedes sat down and asked, "Has he eaten already?"

The housekeeper set a plate of cut fruit and a toasted gluten-free bagel in front of her. "Be sure and have some of that fresh butter from our cows, and the honey from our local bees," she said. "And I made the blackberry jam, no iffy stuff, just real food. Yes, Cowboy was up earlier than usual and ate before I got here. I'm not sure what he's workin' on. He canceled his schedule today; told me he was helpin' a friend."

Lacey came in, greeting them both and meeting Louisa before plopping down to a plate set for her. Louisa turned off the Bible study on a small tablet propped on the counter and chatted with them about her family, and as they were finishing, Cowboy came in. He asked how they slept, if there was anything they needed, and then announced that he would take their bags to the cars when they were ready.

Cowboy was solemn today. Mercedes studied his face. "Do you and Annette have a plan for when we meet at the cottage?" she ventured.

He nodded and replied, "She stayed at Margie's house last night when she got in for a few hours of rest. Margie is the caretaker. We'll meet them at the cottage in about half an hour."

He held her eyes before turning toward the hallway. And as she went to brush her teeth and get her purse, she knew he had not said all he could have.

No one would imagine that things were not idyllic at Seashell Cottage that morning when they arrived. It was as lovely as it had been yesterday when Mercedes saw it for the first time, refined, graceful and charming, like a Southern Belle. Only her unsettling memory of how someone had gotten inside and left the black cabinet there could mar her visit to this beautiful property today.

As she opened the door of her Jeep, Cowboy was telling Annette to stay in the driveway. She walked up as Lacey and her mother hugged, then Lacey turned to Margie for a hug while Annette greeted Mercedes and introduced her to Margie.

Cowboy squatted at a spot along the front walk, and the ladies grew quiet, watching him snap photos where the ground was disturbed. When he seemed satisfied, he asked Annette for the key to the front door. They ambled to the porch while she fidgeted with the key on a ring with others to get it off. When she gave it to him, they started speaking too low together for anyone to hear.

Studying the porch as carefully as he had done with the walkway, Cowboy pointed out a few things to Annette, who shook her head and turned to call for Margie. She waved them all to come join her.

"Margie, have you seen this scuff mark on the porch?" Cowboy indicated a black mark on the wood.

The housekeeper peered closely at the mark, then leaned over to examine it. Shaking her head, she replied, "I can't account for every scratch, and a postal delivery could have made this. But I sweep the porch every week and just did that the day before Lacey was comin'. I hope I would've noticed this, to clean it up, but I didn't."

He nodded slowly and rose, turning his attention to the front door, and stopped cold. After a few moments, he snapped another photo and turned to the ladies. "Lacey, did you leave a key in the front door yesterday?"

Mercedes saw that Lacey did not comprehend what Cowboy was saying. So, she said, "Lacey and I did not even look at the front door yesterday. When I arrived, we walked around the garden area and to the back door. She was checking on the bird baths for Margie."

Annette went to stand beside him and studied the door before looking up at Cowboy. "We all have our house keys. How could this be?"

Shaking his head, the investigator started looking over the door frame. "What about the fabric fibers on this hinge?" he asked. "Margie, did you brush up against the open door, or shake out any rugs or other fabric?"

Margie looked at him as if he had asked if she had visited another planet lately, and Mercedes had to bite her lips to keep from grinning. The housekeeper said, "I don't recall bumping into the door or using a cloth to clean it. But I certainly didn't shake out a rug or drapes or anything here—not on the front porch where we greet guests!"

Lacey giggled and Annette hid a smile with her hand. A lopsided smile tugged at Cowboy's mouth as he put on gloves and took tweezers and a small clear bag from his pocket. He pulled fibers from the hinge, as evidence so miniscule that Mercedes knew he had experience knowing how to search for it.

After tucking the bag into his pocket, the investigator turned to the door lock. He touched the key in the lock to slide it out, then he backed up to the sunlight and studied it.

Annette came to see, and they exchanged looks. "There has never been a black key to this front door," she said. "Never. I know you can make them in all colors at the grocery or hardware stores, but I have never done so and would never choose black."

Cowboy handed her his phone and asked her to take a photo of the key in the sunlight against his white glove. Then he told them to stay behind him while he inserted it again into the lock.

In her mind, Mercedes again heard the words that had troubled her yesterday.

Expect the unexpected from an unseen enemy.

She caught her breath and took a step back. The others were following Cowboy to make their way through the open door. "Wait!" she blurted, reaching for Lacey's arm.

Lacey stopped short. Cowboy stuck his arm out to block them, but it was too late for Margie. She looked past him and cried out in dismay, pointing at something. "A root!" she gasped. "There's a root on the chandelier!"

"Stay here!" Cowboy ordered, and Mercedes pulled Lacey back with her so Margie would not knock her over in her retreat from the open door. Annette reached for Margie's hand and scolded her.

"Hey, now, none of that nonsense," she said. "You know those things have no power over Christians."

Baffled, Lacey looked wide-eyed at them. "What are you talking about? What's wrong?"

Margie clamped one hand up to her mouth with wide eyes fixed on Annette. Still gripping Margie's other hand under the shade of the front verandah, Annette looked at her daughter and answered.

"Margie and I are old enough to remember the time here in Beaufort when Frogmore was one of the most powerful voodoo centers in America. I don't know how to prove such a claim."

The caretaker dropped the hand she held over her trembling lips and said, "Even as recent as back in 1997, bad things happened to people who had a root curse on them."

Nodding at her and squeezing her hand, Annette said, "Yes, but remember, those so-called curses were removed by yet another root. So mostly, do you agree with me that a root could be good or bad to people who believed in their power?"

Margie sighed and wiped her hand over her brow. "Yes, of course."

Annette continued, saying, "In the Bible, Jesus went around reversing many curses, and he drove out demons. Because we belong to him now, we are sacred space, protected by his power."

"It was just so sudden, I reacted as I did when I was little," said Margie. "It was a shock. I know what you say is true, but something feels off about this place today. Makes me nervy."

"You're right," said Annette. "Let's work together to learn why that thing is here, and how that key and cabinet got here, and what all this means."

Margie stood straighter and looked hopeful. "Yes! Maybe someone put the root here because in their beliefs, this root cancels the curse of the cabinet," she offered.

Annette looked interested, but doubtful. "Okay, that's a possibility. But that means people are getting into this house, with a key, and you told me you have not left an extra key anywhere to find."

"Right, I didn't," said Margie, puckering her brow. "But all this has made me remember something odd that happened a couple of weeks ago, Annette. I was helping with the catering at a fancy local fundraising dinner and went back to move my car, but it was gone. My keys were in it because my hands were full, carrying trays of food, and a young guy hired from the local college carried coolers for me. Another young man said valets had moved it to make room for the trailer to unload more tables and chairs. That scared me. I went to look for it in the parking lot for vendors, and it was there, keys inside. Nothing was suspicious in the car until I handled my keys and noticed that they were out of order. They were all there, but out of order. I moved the seashell printed one for this house back where I keep it."

Annette scowled. "Margie, this is important," she said. "You need to tell Cowboy about it."

Lacey stretched out a hand and wailed, "What is a *root*?"

Mercedes blurted, "It's a token, Lacey, made by a witch or a root doctor. He can't practice medicine without a license, so he creates charms and powders—nothing to be consumed. The charms are shaped like a little carrot and made of flannel fabric in different colors. He stuffs them with a secret concoction he makes up, leaving a thin root trailing out from the tip."

"He stuffs 'em with terrible things like the heart of an owl or frog's feet, crushed bone, or dirt taken from a graveyard at midnight," Margie added. She turned a guilty glance at Annette and said, "Or, so they claim. We don't know if they contain anything but weeds."

Lacey balked and took a step back. Mercedes struggled not to smile. Annette's tone was soothing when she said to her daughter, "So go the tales that the witch or root doctors tell. People hide these root tokens near an object or person to curse or bless it effectively. But no one knows what the result of all that will be. No matter what the intention behind the root was, whatever happened was open to interpretation. So even if a proper spell was cast, a Christian can bring the matter up with Jesus. He reverses curses!"

She looked at Mercedes, hopefully, for any helpful comment. Mercedes nodded and said, "There's a verse in the Bible about curses, and in my line of work, I thought it was wise to remember it. I think it's Proverbs 26:2. It says an undeserved curse goes nowhere. It will be like a fluttering sparrow or a darting swallow."

At the first mention of the Bible, Lacey glanced away. But when she understood how appropriate the verse was, she looked back at Mercedes, questioning with raised brows. Mercedes smiled and nodded.

They all turned to the verandah as Cowboy filled the doorway and stepped out. "I took down the root, and the house seems to be fine," he said, walking toward them. "I can't find any footprints, no evidence anyone came inside, other than these items. They were careful to clean up all traces of their identity. Stay out here a minute."

He paused as Margie reached out for his arm. Her eyes searched his face as if making sure he was unscathed by a curse. "What—what did you do with it, Cowboy?"

His expression was gentle, but his words were matter of fact. "It's evidence, Margie. I can't destroy it yet. But I assure you, I prayed over it, and I'm putting it in my truck for now."

"No!" Annette blurted out, stepping toward him. "Put it in my car, Chris. This is about me and my family, not you. I shouldn't have dragged you into this."

Cowboy looked down at her for a few silent moments, then answered. "Yes, it's about you and your family, and you don't have a clue how to deal with this. I do. That's why you called me and that's why I'm taking it. I know who to see and my source will recognize the signature style of the witch who made it. You did the right thing."

He smiled and started walking toward his truck. Lacey watched him, then turned to her mother's puckered look of concern. "A witch?" she squeaked. "Roots, curses, black cabinets—Mama, will you please tell me what in the world is going on?"

Chapter 5

As Annette, Lacey, Margie, and Mercedes waited on the front walkway of Seashell Cottage, Annette smoothed her expression and reached up to push back a wayward lock of her daughter's hair. "Lacey, I hoped to wait until you were much older to tell you about some family history," she said in a soft voice. "But the Lord has his own timetable and purposes, and it looks like he chose now to be the right time."

Cowboy walked back to them after putting the root in his truck. Annette turned to him and said, "I need some time with Lacey and Mercedes before we go in. Do you mind helping Margie get around to the kitchen through the back porch, so she doesn't have to walk under the chandelier or by the cabinet? She has something to tell you about her key to the house. And Margie, if you have lemons in the refrigerator, would you mind making us all some lemonade?"

Cowboy smiled and nodded to Margie. As they all turned to walk around to the back, Mercedes said, "Cowboy, as Lacey and I were leaving the house yesterday to go to lunch, I caught a movement behind the hedge. Over there," she said, pointing. "I didn't get a clear sight of the figure. When the person noticed he or she had been seen, they jerked back out of sight."

They all looked in the direction of the evergreen shrubbery she pointed to and Cowboy said, "You didn't feel threatened?"

Mercedes considered this, then shook her head. "No," she said, her eyes fixed on his. "I was just aware, not afraid."

She glanced at Lacey. "Lacey was talking about where to go for lunch, and I saw no need to alarm her, so I said nothing.

I forgot about it until we found the house had been invaded again."

Annette sighed. "Another mystery for you to investigate, Cowboy." Then she said, "Lacey's favorite place is the old Summer House. Mercedes, Lacey, and I will be out there in the garden when you need us again."

Things were happening fast. Too fast. Mercedes felt unsettled and uncertain about what she was doing here. She hesitated as the group started walking, wondering how she ended up in this situation.

With her first slow step to follow her client and her client's daughter, she prayed silently. *Jesus, what is my role here?*

The prayer was how she confirmed her own discomfort, as if Jesus missed that part. Under her breath, she whispered, "I know. I'm here because you opened the door."

If she had learned anything in life, it was that each adventure she stumbled through prepared her to understand a bigger picture that the Lord wanted her to see. Now, she wondered what he was working on to bring order to this mess she found herself in.

It was easy to understand why Lacey's favorite spot was the Summer House at Shell Cottage. Part of the charm of this gazebo was the romantic architecture. A dreamy small garden that embraced it, with a seashell pathway through flora and fauna that showcased colorful blooms all year round. Mercedes inhaled a deep, calming breath of the white gardenias, wondering if there could be any better flowers for a romantic setting such as this one.

Pausing a moment, she touched a velvety fragile petal nestled in the brilliant green foliage. But Annette's voice from the steps of the gazebo made her look up and crunch the white shells underfoot on her way to join her and her daughter.

"I named Lacey for the ornamental designs on the woodwork here in the Summer House," Annette told her.

"What a sweet connection!" Mercedes said, looking up to admire the intricate lace trim work pattern of a skilled woodcrafter. She followed Annette's wave of her hand in an invitation to sit in an oversized rocking chair made for comfort. Annette and Lacey sat together in a generous sized swing that was suspended from a large beam in the vaulted ceiling.

"Is there a story behind your name, too?" asked Lacey.

Drawing in another breath of the fragrant gardenias in the warm summer air, Mercedes settled deeper into the rocking chair and tried to relax. "Oh, yes," she answered. "The nutshell version is that my namesake was my great grand aunt, who lived in England."

"She must have been special," Lacey remarked, wriggling into a comfortable position beside her mother.

"Yes, she was. I found one of her journals and I'm getting to know her, in a way. But it was her beloved grandmother, Claire, who was legendary in that country," Mercedes mused. Then she wondered why she had revealed this to acquaintances.

"You're more like Claire, I think," Annette said. Mercedes caught her breath and met Annette's eyes, then swallowed and blushed. Speechless, she glanced away and rocked her chair for a few moments in silence, remembering what happened at

Majestic Oaks Plantation when she used Claire's small silver dagger.

"Well," said Annette. She cleared her throat. "I promised an explanation for the strange circumstances we face today. I want both of you to understand that never for a moment would I have brought you into this, if I had any idea what would happen. It unnerves me that someone in my family's past knew my daughter was coming here to live."

With a deep sigh, she turned to look at Seashell Cottage. "I don't even know where to begin."

Lacey said, "I do, Mama. Tell us about the cabinet."

Her mother's face darkened, and she grimaced. "Yes. That horrible cabinet."

Life went on as usual for a late summer day in the Lowcountry. Around the grounds and gazebo at Seashell Cottage, tourists strolled by, studying their guidebooks and taking photos from under the shade of their sun hats. Slow traffic became busier as the lunch hour drew near.

But Mercedes became engrossed in the remarkable, tragic, yet triumphant account of her client's life. Annette said, "The first time I laid eyes on the Devil's Drawer was in my father's funeral home."

Lacey gasped and Mercedes froze in her rocking chair. "The—the devil's drawer?" Lacey stuttered. "In a funeral home? Are you saying your father was—that he worked in a funeral home?"

Mercedes felt her heart jump, then sink. She grappled with where this conversation was going.

Annette nodded to answer Lacey's question, then her hand moved to rest on the heavy chain that suspended the swing. Her eyes took on a faraway look as she stared at the garden. "I can't remember why we stopped after school that day—my mother, older brother, and I," she began. "My brother told me later that my mom had to check with my father about something right away and he would not be home until late. This was before cellphones. She couldn't wait until he got her message from the receptionist and called home. We rarely went to the funeral home because my dad didn't like us to be there. I was only ten, and I forgot I was never allowed to go beyond the lobby. My brother went to sit down and picked up a magazine while my mother stood at the reception desk and asked if my father was available to speak to her."

Her knuckles whitened as she squeezed her fingers around the chain of the swing, and she said, "I didn't like the stark lines of the black-and-white checkered tile lobby floor, but I played a game on them, stepping from one square to the other. My father's voice came from a room down the hall. For a while afterwards, I blamed myself for what happened. That's what children do, you know. But my mother, brother, and grandparents helped me understand. It was time for secrets to come to light."

She paused and relaxed her grip on the cool metal links before she spoke again. "I did not know of the work that goes on in a mortuary, or about funeral related services. In my mind, my father was like solemn pastors I saw on television speaking to grieving loved ones. He offered comfort in what they called a receiving and at funerals. He dealt with taking care of things they shouldn't worry about at such a time, like limousines, flowers, and scriptures about heaven."

"But Mama, you told me you didn't know your father," Lacey said.

Annette turned to look at her, nodding. "That's true, I didn't, honey. He owned the funeral home and mortuary, and sometimes, there weren't enough employees on shifts. Other nights, he had mysterious meetings he couldn't talk about. When he was home, I always felt that we only saw the man he wanted us to think he was."

Lacey's brow puckered in concentration. "Was he upset the day you went down the hall?" she asked.

Annette reached for her daughter's hand and gently rocked the swing again. She looked off into the distance, remembering. "Yes," she almost whispered. Then, she told Lacey and Mercedes what happened when she went to find her father, and her nose itched because of some strange smells. At an open door, she stopped to look inside. Dread washed over her when she saw a sheet draped over what must have been a deceased child on a table. The sound of her father's voice speaking to a woman in the room frightened her. The woman was putting a box into her purse.

And then Annette saw the black cabinet.

Sitting in the swing with her daughter in the summerhouse, telling her story, Annette's voice trembled with emotion. Her hand flew to her face and covered her eyes. Mercedes and Lacey glanced at each other with grim faces and waited until she could speak again. When she did, she was pale, but calm.

"Something was terribly wrong," she said. "Something a child could sense but not understand. The sight of that cabinet stunned me so much that it dominated my attention. I don't remember what the woman said to my father, but when he answered her, it was in a tone of voice I had never heard him use, so I listened. He told her he had never agreed to this. She told him to ask his lodge leader if he doubted her. Then the woman noticed me. All I can remember is that I was terrified and got goosebumps."

Lacey leaned closer to her mother and touched her arm. "Was it the way she looked, or something she said?" she asked.

Shaking her head, Annette said, "I believe it was her eyes, her oily demeanor, and a slow, wicked grin. She was oddly attractive and cat-like, but if it's true that our eyes are the windows to our souls, her soul was evil. My dad turned to look at what distracted her. When he saw me, so many emotions crossed his face. I will never forget that moment. Shock, love, fear, and resolve were all there. The resolve was the one that I understood best. Nothing was ever going to be the same again."

She blinked against tears and sniffed. "Well, I guess I blocked out most of what happened after that, and time has a way of erasing memories. I remember my father pulled my arm toward that black-and-white checkered lobby, where my mother was just searching for me. Her expression when she saw the strange woman frightened me further, and she grabbed me from my dad. The look that passed between them was that same resolve I understood as a point of no return. Later, my brother told me he had rushed from his seat in the lobby to my mom and that she told him to take me to the car. He said he stayed with me, calming me."

"Oh, Mama," Lacey said. "Grandy Anna had a divorce. All I ever heard hinted at was that her husband was unfaithful."

"Yes. My dad never came home again. My brother told me that soon after this, incriminating photos released in the news suggested my father was having an affair. This opened the way for my mother to divorce him, and we moved here to Seashell Cottage to live with my grandparents."

She smiled at Lacey and Mercedes. "I soon had a stepfather who was a good bit older than my mother but was home every night and weekend," she said. "Don't be sad for me, Lacey. Your Grampy loved me and my brother as if we were his own, and I was so happy here. My life was full of love, laughter, family togetherness, friends, and church activities! But my brother was older and could remember a time before our biological father grew distant from us. Though he was happy here, he wanted to know more about what happened that day that changed our lives. He would hide things he learned from my mother. While he was in college, he died in a bizarre car accident. Later, I learned that losing a child isn't uncommon in families linked to the associations my father had."

Mercedes stilled her rocking chair, squeezed her eyes shut and drew a deep breath. Her client's story confirmed her suspicions about the black cabinet, but she had hoped she was wrong.

When she opened her eyes, they were full of compassion for Annette, who she found was watching her. "You understand, don't you?" Annette asked.

Nodding, Mercedes whispered, "Yes. But I don't know what to say except I'm so sorry."

"Thank you," Annette said. "It was so tragic, yes, if that was the end of the story. But it was not, and the enemy did not win. Later, my father learned he was dying, and he contacted me.

It was a shock, but I have a solid Christian support system of family and friends who helped. I examined the past through the eyes of an adult. Then, I traveled to meet him."

She looked at Mercedes. "You may have heard accounts from nurses who sit with dying patients, some of whom are in secret organizations. They claim these people kick and scream before they pass on. I don't know. All I can say is that this did not happen to my father, because he no longer belonged to one. I am blessed by his own riveting testimony of learning what he was into. After breaking down to confide in a local pastor, one of only a few that he trusted, he left it all behind. His pastor friend encouraged him to reconcile with me. So, he wrote a very long letter in case I wouldn't come to see him, or if he was too sick to speak. But I arrived, and he could take my hand and tell me most of this himself and put the letter in my hand. My father had surrendered his life to Jesus, repented of all the horrific death oaths he had sworn to, and he had no other god. He knew I was a believer, too."

"Oh, Mama," Lacey whispered, looking as if she was going to cry. Her voice caught as she added, "This is so heartbreaking! Think of all those wasted years."

Mercedes remembered the small package of tissues in her cross-body bag, and she quickly reached for it. As she rose to hand the tissue pack to Lacey, she met Annette's sad eyes and said, "Annette, what did your father do with the business?"

"Don't worry, he did not leave that to me in his will," Annette assured her. "In fact, my father simply donated the funeral home and its contents to a local medical university. He died with nothing, but he left no bills unpaid. In his letter, he wrote that he would not pass on any of the devil's property or money to me. In the associations he was part of, funeral homes and death are big business. His pastor came daily to the hospice center to talk about the Bible and pray with him, and he handled the arrangements for his care and a very simple burial. There was nothing for me to do but sit with him for several days until he went peacefully to join Jesus."

The three women sat silent for a few minutes, mulling the story over, soothed by the swing and rocking chair movements. "Annette, did your father ever mention the black cabinet?" Mercedes asked. "Was it part of the donation to the medical school?"

Annette shrugged. "He only referred to it in his letter. He wrote that on the day I stood in the doorway, he knew he must cut all ties with us to move forward. He had to pay off the loan for the business, which he owed to his connections at his lodge. The woman I saw was there to collect a tribute from him for 'ceremonies.' She called herself a witch, but he didn't take her seriously at first. The black cabinet was an important furnishing from a secret room at his lodge, and he had to put offerings into what he called the Devil's Drawer and lock it. I don't know if that was the real name for it, but he called it that. He had moved into a new level of commitment, and he did as he was told."

"Mama, that makes no sense!" wailed Lacey. "You said that day you saw love passing over his face when he looked at you. How could he leave his family? What was he doing?"

Annette wrapped her arm around Lacey. "Honey, I waited until you were older to tell you these things. By the time he died, I was old enough to see with the heart and experience of an adult and be reunited with him. Maybe you will come to accept them, too. My father made a serious mistake that could mean ruin and prison, or worse, and expose the truth about his organization. Unless he separated himself from us, we were in danger, too. There is no place where this powerful group has no influence. My father never said he knew anything about what happened to my brother, but now I thought I knew. Maybe he had no information that made him a threat to anyone. Maybe all he did was ask inconvenient questions."

"Was he a Christian, Mama?" asked Lacey, knitting her brow.

Her mother smiled and squeezed her hand. "You mean Anthony, my wonderful brother?" She blinked back sudden tears. "Oh, yes, honey, he was. I wish you had known him. And here comes his best friend, Cowboy, with lemonade. I'm ready for some, aren't you?"

Chapter 6

That was the connection, thought Mercedes. Puzzle pieces zinged into their places. Cowboy—Chris Coulter—was Annette's big brother's best friend when he was alive. Best friends share interests and secrets. Cowboy knew better than Annette what her family history was and may have aided her brother in learning the truth. He had remained close to the Ladson family and to Annette.

Does he have an unfulfilled promise to keep? She wondered. *Did Anthony confide in him about his fears about Annette?*

She studied the lanky man as he grinned and offered them clear insulated cups of pale lemonade with lemonade ice floating inside. Dainty cocktail umbrellas were stuck into floating stacks of strawberries and lemon slices. The tray was woven white wicker with a bottom of mauve shades of a glass mosaic and seashells.

The ladies were oohing with admiration at Margie's artistry with the drinks as they lifted theirs from the tray. Cowboy turned to Mercedes' chair. She reached for her cup and napkin as Annette was telling them that Margie had a part-time job helping a caterer, and that she had a talent for creative food presentations.

As Mercedes looked up to thank Cowboy, he nodded, but his warm hazel eyes were studying hers. *He's trying to gauge my reaction to Annette's revelation,* she thought. *Or is he looking for signs that I can help?*

Cowboy eased into another rocking chair in the gazebo, dangling the wicker tray nonchalantly by the handle. "Margie's making up a lunch, since we're likely to be here a while now, waiting on locks to be changed," he said in his lazy voice. "Can I tell her how things are going out here?"

"Do you know what my uncle Anthony found out that may have gotten him killed?" blurted Lacey. "Did he tell you what his father was putting into the Devil's Drawer?"

Mercedes stopped as she was about to take another sip of Margie's delicious lemonade. Her eyes darted to Cowboy's face.

Startled, Annette opened her mouth but exchanged a look with Cowboy and shut it again. Lacey had emerged from being a young lady who needed comfort to one who was ready for answers.

Only a blink of Cowboy's eyes registered any surprise at these abrupt questions. He remained relaxed, but a muscle in his jaw flexed while he collected his thoughts. He rocked in his chair for a few moments of silence, then he said, "The investigation and autopsy revealed no evidence that your uncle was murdered, Lacey." As far as we know, something distracted him, and he ran his car off the road. His injuries were fatal."

"But he had been on the trail of understanding what was going on with his father's business, or the people his father associated with," Lacey reminded him. "Mama told me you were once in law enforcement. Do you agree with the accident report?"

Now, Cowboy looked down at the floor. Slowly, he shook his head. "No, Lacey, I can't say I do. I got into law enforcement to investigate unusual cases like that one, but I soon learned that only a small percentage of officers aren't part of their own secret organization. They take care of each other, and I would never fit in. This limited my work and often left my hands tied."

He raised his head to look at Lacey and told her, "So, I studied to become an attorney, and I became an independent investigator with professional contacts. I only work with law enforcement when I have the facts about cases to submit, and we understand one another. There's still no guarantee that the guilty will not get aid or walk free."

Annette squeezed her daughter's hand and said, "Now you see why I called Cowboy about the break-in here at Seashell Cottage when most people would have called the local police. I am not confident in a truthful resolution about a crime involving my family because of my father and brother. And no harm has come to anyone except for fear of someone having a key to the house. We will change locks this afternoon, right, Cowboy?"

"I've called a locksmith and handyman to be here soon," Cowboy said. "And Lacey, we will have doorbell cameras installed, and timers for outdoor lighting as well. Next week, I'll come here to meet with a security camera team. It will be a lot more complicated from today onward if anyone attempts to get inside again."

Turning to her mother, Lacey said, "Daddy won't be back home from his business trip until next week. Can you stay until at least Monday, Mama?"

"Of course," Annette said, lifting her daughter's hand and giving it a fleeting kiss. "That's what I have planned. I will stay until I believe you are settled and safe.

"Thank you!" Lacey breathed, leaning against her mother's shoulder. "Maybe you'll remember more things from the past that can help me understand all this. I believe whoever went to all the trouble to get a copy of the house key or to pick the lock knew I would be arriving. They knew I would tell you about the cabinet, and you would rush here. How is that information about me available? Few people knew. And why torment you with the black cabinet? Why bring the Devil's Drawer to Seashell Cottage? Your father cut ties with you, then with his group, or club, or whatever he was into."

"People who want to know things and have the right connections don't need to search long to find out," Cowboy said, looking down at the tray as he switched hands to dangle it. "I want to tell you something important. You won't grasp how significant this is until later, but don't forget it. You can't afford to forget it."

Then he looked up, meeting each of their eyes as he looked around. "This includes you, too, Mercedes. Never forget that blood is supernatural currency."

Annette closed her eyes and sighed. Lacey whispered, "What?"

It was Mercedes who broke the silence with a solemn nod and saying, "In the Bible, and all over the world since ancient times, blood is sacred. Especially human blood. People bear the image of God, so the consequences of spilling human blood, even from a wild animal, were severe. According to the Bible, life is in the blood. Our DNA, our genetics, our family bloodline are in it. Jesus' blood is vital as an ultimate sacrifice to cover our sin, ending the need for the symbolic shedding of the blood of animals. So, in the occult, blood is spiritually charged, a necessity in many rituals."

Cowboy nodded, cleared his throat, then added, "Throughout history, the gods of pagans have required blood sacrifices. And with today's technology, it is used to corrupt humans, such as creating hybrid beings."

Lacey drew a quick breath. Wide-eyed, she said, "I learned this in science class in college. Isn't this about progress in health?"

"You'll be hearing more about it in the news," said Cowboy. "The world is racing to improve on humans by manipulating their genetics and integrating them into machines. And as to your other question about the Devil's Drawer, if your uncle found that out, he did not have time to tell me before he died. I want to believe it was money, the way mafia mob bosses demand a fee from businesspeople that they control. In my work and in the Bible, there are territorial powers, including witches and warlocks, and they are authorities over these secret groups. They work spells and rituals to manipulate events to go their way. This is not a fairy tale or a fantasy story, Lacey. It's not a fictional horror story. This is life on Earth. Once you know about it, you will see it everywhere."

Mercedes' mind flashed a recent memory of news about convictions for what mortuary employees had sold online, and she hoped money was the only thing Annette's father had ever locked in the Devil's Drawer. Like Cowboy, she was unwilling to imagine anything else.

A car door slammed from the driveway. Instantly, Cowboy was on his feet and down the steps of the summerhouse, clutching the heavy wicker tray. With a restraining wave of his hand, he motioned for the ladies to stay where they were.

Annette sighed. "What now?" she said, and her voice betrayed both her wariness and her weariness. She had traveled to Beaufort from Florida and had little sleep before arriving at the house.

"At least no one is sneaking around," Mercedes offered. "The visitor knows there are four vehicles in the driveway."

Soon, a pleasant young male voice answered Cowboy's greeting, and as the voices grew louder, the women knew he was bringing a guest to meet them. As the two men turned the corner into the garden, Mercedes was surprised to see the young man she had watched during lunch yesterday. Today, he carried a beautiful bouquet of bright flowers.

"These lovely ladies are Mrs. Annette Ladson, her daughter Miss Lacey Ladson, and Mercedes, who is a friend helping them with some details about the historic value of Seashell Cottage," said Cowboy, making the introductions. "And ladies, this gentleman is a local named Spencer Wadell. He will be working with Lacey, and he wanted to stop by with a welcome gift."

Spencer grinned and almost stammered as he spoke. "Uh, Miss Ladson, I'm sorry if it's awkward to stop like this. You see, I was uncertain if it was appropriate to bring a welcome gift to the office. Some women—well, they aren't open to that sort of gesture. But Cowboy assured me you would love these."

He held out the bouquet to Lacey, who beamed and stood as she nodded. As Spencer mounted the stairs and Lacey held out her arms for the flowers, Annette moved to the rocking chair that Cowboy had left empty.

"Please come sit with us, Spencer," she said, waving toward the seat beside her daughter on the swing.

"Oh, thank you, Mrs. Ladson," Spencer said as he steadied the swing to ensure Lacey was settled in it before taking the seat beside her. "The shade here helps against the heat of the day."

"Yes, it does, and we'll need to escape to the air conditioning soon," Annette said. "A friend in the house made us fresh lemonade and Cowboy—uh, Chris—brought it out on that tray. Would you like any?"

Spencer glanced at Cowboy, who looked relaxed as he leaned against the railing of the gazebo. "Oh, no, please, I don't want to be any trouble and I'll only be a few minutes," he said. "I have an appointment soon."

Then he turned to Lacey. "I didn't realize you knew Cowboy, or I'd have introduced myself yesterday," he said. "When I saw you and your friend in town at lunch, I recognized you from your photo on your resume. We will be working together, and everyone at the office is excited to have you join our team."

Lacey's voice conveyed her surprised delight. "Oh," she said prettily, and then she blushed and leaned her face down to inhale the fragrance of her bouquet. "You don't know how much I needed to hear that, and it means a lot to me, Spencer. Thank you."

It was Spencer's turn to beam back at her, and he said, "My pleasure. Oh, and my business card is in that little envelope." He pointed at the paper tucked into the ribbon encasing the flowers and ending in a bow. "You know, just in case you need anything."

Mercedes smiled as she watched this exchange, and she wanted to applaud Annette's wisdom when Annette asked

Spencer if he was related to the Wadell family in town that attended her church.

"Oh, yes ma'am, I am!" he exclaimed. "I go there, too. My grandparents have lived in Beaufort for a couple of decades now, and I have splendid memories of visiting them. But they are aging, and my dad worries about them. He can't retire yet, and my mother is committed to helping her mother there at home, so he was grateful I wanted to live here after college. I check on my grandparents every day, and I even taught them to use a computer tablet to text me. Teaching them to video call me is taking some time, though."

Cowboy said he needed to go back inside and check on Margie's progress with lunch, and he shook hands with Spencer as they exchanged farewells. Then Spencer, too, said his interruption had been long enough.

As he rose, they all stood, and he reached for Lacey's hand. "I hope I'll see you at church on Sunday and the office on Monday," he told her. "Until then, don't forget about my card. Call if you need anything at all, like the other night with that late furniture delivery. I'd feel better knowing you weren't here alone."

Halfway to the back door, Cowboy spun back on his heel to face the group. "Spencer, did you see a furniture delivery to Seashell Cottage?" he asked.

The young man raised his brows and nodded. "Well, yeah. There was an issue with a broken air conditioner in one of our properties and the repairman had a full schedule that day," he replied. "He would come out for after-hours prices, but I was the only person available to meet him. It was late when I drove by here. Maybe ten or eleven o'clock?"

Cowboy asked the ladies to check on Margie and see if she needed any help with lunch, and again, they invited Spencer to stay. The young man glanced at his watch and seemed regretful that he could not. But he asked if he could stop back by if he could get away.

Lacey thanked him for his thoughtful gesture to come by with flowers. As he walked back to the driveway with Cowboy, Mercedes heard him answering questions about describing the delivery truck he saw two nights before. Then she told Annette she must check in with Quincy, who was waiting for a call, and that she would come inside soon.

When Quincy answered, his voice was breathy. She heard him jogging out of range of the rest of his team, whose voices faded away. "Hey, babe, I was just going to check my phone to see if you sent any photos of that cabinet you talked about," he said. "Everything okay?"

Mercedes found she did not know where to begin. "Well, I am okay, yes. Um, we have been here at the house since mid-morning, but something else happened before we made it inside and Cowboy needed to take care of it. So, I've been sitting in a garden gazebo with the Ladson family to hear some history about the cabinet, and then a new friend stopped by with flowers for Lacey. He witnessed the delivery of that cabinet I told you about, though he does not know there's anything wrong with that. Hopefully, I will get some photos for you after lunch."

Quincy's voice was puzzled when he asked what this meant. "And what kept you outside in the heat?" he said.

She felt drained and blurted, "Oh, Quincy! I wish you were here. You grew up with all this bizarre stuff about blood and secret societies. I have zero desire to know more than I already did about these things, but it's raining down on me, and I can no longer pretend it's not an undercurrent in my life." Her voice trembled when she said, "They need someone knowledgeable and steady, like you."

"Blood? What's this about blood? Are you trying to tell me the cabinet belongs to an occult group?"

Mercedes nodded, then remembered he could not see her answer. "Yes," she exclaimed. "And one feature in it is called the Devil's Drawer!"

Quincy gasped. Then, his groan of frustration came across the phone, and she winced. In normal situations, her fiancé was suave and steady.

"I'm overreacting, Quincy," she said, calming her voice. "Strange things keep popping into my day and I'm just—you know, off kilter. Let me tell you the main points and if you have time, you can think through them. I could use any suggestions that will help us, but you may need to text them to me. Lunch will be ready soon. Quincy?"

"Yeah?" he asked.

"Thank you for listening, and for praying," she said.

He guffawed. "You're welcome, beautiful, but there's not much else I can do from here."

Chapter 7

Quincy Holmwood put his cell phone in a pocket of his khaki utility shorts, then he pulled a blue bandana from around his neck. It might have helped against sweat when he put it on that morning, but now it felt as wet as his brow when he dragged it across his forehead.

He looked back at the white canopy tent where he had been sorting the last of the artifacts before this phase of the archaeological dig site in St. Augustine, Florida, would end. The sponsor had what it needed for now to raise more money for the next phase and soon, Quincy would be wrapping up his contribution and moving on to the next job.

No, not immediately, he remembered. There was the matter of winning his grandparents over about his engagement to Mercedes. And maybe his dad, though his father's resistance dissolved significantly last week in Bluffton, when he realized he had wronged her years ago on the dig in Peru, in fear and to hide the truth from his project sponsors.

Quincy's steps toward his trailer were slow and deliberate, but his mind was racing, turning over the things Mercedes had told him. He had sent the rest of the team off to lunch. Now, he needed time alone to think and to open the small refrigerator. He had to empty it out by tomorrow before leaving.

When he opened the trailer door, the air conditioning flowed over him like cool water. He raised a silent thanks for this blessing as he went to the sink to wash up, and while he was at it, he asked Jesus to bless his coming meal. As he scrubbed up to his elbows and washed his face, the things Mercedes had told him turned around in the back of his mind, like puzzle pieces trying to find the right fit.

Something familiar lurked around the pieces, waiting to come to light. That bothered him more than the things she said.

Glancing at his watch and peering out the window of his trailer to see if any of the team was back at the dig site, Quincy chewed the last bite of a roast beef sandwich. He had about twenty minutes to make a phone call, and longer if the typical afternoon shower poured down.

Reaching for one of his ever-present notebooks and a pen, he started jotting down notes from his conversation with Mercedes. Then he fished for his phone in a pocket and settled into an upholstered chair. As he waited for his father to answer, he jotted down another note on the page.

"Quincy, it's good to hear from you. Are you having lunch?" asked his father.

"Yes, and I'm cooling off in the trailer," answered Quincy. "We're tying up the loose ends with reports, and I hope to wrap up here tomorrow. How is everyone at home?"

"We're great, nothing to report," said his father. "Your mom and grandmother are at the hair salon, then they plan to do some shopping. Your grandfather has a new fishing buddy a few houses down and they're out all afternoon. I'm clearing off paperwork on my desk."

"Do you have a few minutes for some questions?" Quincy asked. "Your experience is a faster resource than searching online."

"Sure," replied his dad with a note of interest. "What are you working on?"

"I remember that you and Granddad interacted with friends and family who were in secret societies," Quincy began. "You once said that witchcraft spell casting is the basis of rituals in Lucifer worship, and that these are foundational to these organizations. Are the two linked?"

His father seemed taken aback, then chuckled before saying, "Wow, what a topic! You must be reading one of those blockbuster adventures about secret societies. They do have some interesting fictional takes on religions in archaeology settings, but they contain some truth, too, I'm sorry to say. Any religion or practice that uses spell casting is witchcraft, even if it's a person wearing jewelry that is supposed to ward off evil spirits. Witchcraft is simple. It tries to manipulate circumstances to the benefit of a person at the detriment of others, and it always, always, always costs something in the supernatural realm."

Quincy hesitated, feeling guilty that his father believed he was reading a novel about secret societies involved in archaeology. "Yeah, that makes sense. Do witches and warlocks have a spiritual territory that gives them authority within or over a secret society? Could they demand offerings or tributes?"

"Absolutely," said his father, warming to the topic and sounding like he did when he was making presentations. "Think of Helena Blavatsky. She was a medium, like the Witch of Endor in the Bible. Her inspiration was her great-grandfather, who was a Freemason and Rosicrucian. He had an entire library of occult books. And if you ever read the not-so-secret old handbooks circulating from these societies, it's shocking that anyone would join after the horrific ceremony they endure and the gruesome death oaths they swear to. Christians, especially, should know better than to swear an oath of loyalty and obedience to a secret master. Not to preach or anything, but as I told my cousin, the Bible says to love the Lord with all your heart and do everything for his glory."

Quincy said, "Yes, and I heard Granddad remind him that the Bible says no one can serve two masters, and that he was choosing to serve a different master than Jesus."

"I remember," said his father. "He was considering membership as an advantage to getting the favor of British peerage. Our titles were through landed gentry and distant relatives with no other heirs, with no secret memberships required. As to your question about tributes, most of these groups are obsessed with death, secrets, and becoming a special class of enlightened people above everyone else. Their books, and the testimonies of former members, tell of blood sacrifices such as pagans did ages ago."

"So, like the Bible says, there's nothing new under the sun," Quincy said, tapping his pen lightly on his leg.

His father snorted. "Only repackaged and rebranded for a new generation. They deceive the public, misrepresenting their symbols, so only those at the top understand what the secrets are. I'm not sure anyone has written those down. These groups infiltrate every place where it's possible to have influence and they play on all sides. Quincy, they even had secret clubs for children to attend, to groom them for membership in adult ones. Your mother's grandmother told her about a product called Ovaltine, which used an orphan girl mascot named

Annie, to promote secret memberships back in the 1930s in America. They enclosed items like badges, bracelets, and decoder rings with occult symbolism on them, and they published comic book style magazines that warned them about never telling the secrets. And society references are in old Disney Mickey cartoons."

"Woah," Quincy said, putting down his pen and rubbing his forehead. "Parents didn't notice?"

His dad sighed. "Like you said, nothing has changed, has it? Occult symbolism is everywhere, and most people are clueless. They copy the hand signs and cover one eye because they saw their favorite movie star do it. Little wonder these societies scorn the general population. They've been serving Lucifer, and he will not share power. The promise of special knowledge is a lie, like Eve believed in the garden of Eden."

"So, considering the Bible verses about not serving two masters, and only to serve Jesus, can a Christian be in one of these societies?" asked Quincy, jotting down notes.

"Why? Why would a Christian be in one? That is the big question," his father replied. "These groups are universalists, with members worshipping false gods, and the Bible tells us not to be linked with unbelievers and false teachers. These members are under oath to support one another, even their criminal activities, which is not what Jesus teaches."

Quincy's father paused. "I'm getting long winded, I know, but this topic irks me. I did a paper about the link with these societies and mythology as my dissertation in college. So, no, Christianity is not compatible with secret oaths at the price of gruesome death, or to secret ceremonies and rituals honoring another god."

"I think I get it now," Quincy said. "Jesus was the last sacrifice needed for salvation. No more blood needs to be shed, and no other god deserves to be honored. No ritual is valid in the Lord's eyes and is an insult to him."

"What situation arose in the book that made you wonder about all this?" asked his father.

Quincy hesitated, then admitted, "I'm trying to help Mercedes, Dad. I was going to tell you before our call ended. An unexpected situation arose with her clients in Beaufort yesterday, and today, she's learned that it ties to a secret society and a black cabinet with Egyptian symbols on it. It has a drawer with a strange lock. She will send me photos this afternoon."

His father hissed in alarm. "What?"

Alert, Quincy sat up straight. Somehow, he sensed his father was not upset that, once again, Mercedes found herself in unsettling circumstances. He elaborated with more details. "The cabinet got delivered to the house when no one was there, and no one should have had a key to get in. The client remembers it from her father's funeral home in Washington."

On the other end of the phone, he could tell his father slammed a drawer and rushed out of his office. His father was breathless. "Is Mercedes disturbed by this cabinet?"

Quincy's brows shot up, and his heart jumped. Was his father accepting that if a place, a situation, a person, or an object upset Mercedes, there was always a good reason?

"That's an understatement," he replied. "Everyone there is agitated, so she's not imagining things. After she and her youngest client encountered the cabinet in a closed drawing room, her client's mother was so upset that she paid Mercedes to stay with her daughter at a friend's house last night. The friend is an investigator with a law degree, a Christian, and he checks out fine."

He paused, listening to the background sounds of his father's movements. Was he searching his office for information about the cabinet?

Silence meant his father was expecting more information, so Quincy related Mercedes' nutshell version to him. "The investigator took Mercedes and her youngest client to the house this morning to search for clues about how someone put the cabinet in the drawing room. They met up with the mother and housekeeper and he gathered some evidence outside, but when he went inside to make sure everything was safe, he found that someone left a curse charm on the chandelier in the foyer. It's called a root, a local voodoo type of thing, with the intention that all who walk under it would be affected. They are subjective, so it could even be a blessing instead of a curse. The point is Mercedes' client felt it was time to tell her daughter the family history about the Devil's Drawer."

Quincy heard a car door slam. "I need the address," his father announced. "You can't get there in time."

A car engine started, and Quincy was on his feet. "You mean—I should be there? Are you saying she's in danger? Dad, what's this about?"

"This is about my unfinished business."

Chapter 8

Lacey polished off a triangle shaped sandwich, made a yummy sound in her throat, and told Margie how good it was. She stopped short of licking her fingers when she noticed her mother was watching. Immediately, she reached for her napkin and grinned sheepishly.

Margie smiled at the compliment and looked at Mercedes. "I wish I'd stocked the kitchen before Lacey arrived, but I expected to go shopping with her."

Shaking her head, Mercedes swallowed her last bite of the sandwich she had planned and packed for a picnic the day she traveled up to Beaufort. "The food I brought from home and kept in a cooler needed to be eaten. But it was much better with the homemade vegetable soup you made. Thanks so much!"

The doorbell rang, and they looked around at one another. Cowboy pushed back his chair and rose, saying it must be the locksmith. Margie gathered dishes on a tray and told the other ladies to stay seated. She had everything in hand to clean up.

"I think the new front door handles and locks are beautiful, Annette," said Mercedes. "I'm glad the hardware store delivered them right away."

Annette nodded with a wry smile, then leaned back from the table. "Cowboy has a lot of connections who owe him favors, and most will jump at a chance to do anything for him. I had been meaning to update all the door hardware, anyway. This humid coastal climate is not kind to metal finishings."

Then she knitted her brow and clasped her hands together. "But I never intended that you would have to sit through all this, Mercedes. If I didn't think you should be here, I would tell you to go home and rest. We can do this tomorrow. Can you begin any of your work here this afternoon with your tablet? I can answer questions if they come up, and you can finish today."

They heard Cowboy's voice in the foyer giving instructions to the workmen, who were told nothing about the cabinet behind the closed door. Mercedes told Annette she would start her work while they waited but would like to take photos of the curious artifact when they opened the door. It was not part of the record of Seashell Cottage, but her fiancé was an expert in antiquities and would be interested in the cabinet.

"Of course, no problem at all. I'd like to know his opinion and what he finds about it. I suppose we will all know more when Cowboy's friend arrives to look for the key to the—to that drawer," answered Annette, her voice trailing off.

Mercedes watched Annette, then kept her voice low to ask if she expected something. "Do you believe it contains a message from or about your father?"

Annette looked at her for a long moment, then almost whispered, as if the crew in the foyer might overhear her. "Yes. Perhaps even about my brother. And there may be a warning concerning my daughter."

Lacey sat still, growing pale and keeping her eyes locked on her mother's face. "You believe I am right, then, about what I said in the summer house," she whispered. "That only family and a couple of friends knew I would be here the day after the cabinet arrived. This is a warning, or a statement, or an invitation, or unfinished business. I believe Cowboy thinks it is about blood."

"I don't know, honey, but I see your point," her mother said. "You've taken all this very well once the initial shock wore off. I'm so proud of you, Lacey."

Lacey's hands shot up to cover her face. Startled, Mercedes met Annette's eyes and saw insight that mothers have. They waited.

"I don't deserve your pride in me, Mama," Lacey said after a few moments. Her voice cracked and she settled her hands in her lap. "I've messed up, and I kept making excuses not to go to church while I was in college. I'm not even a Christian. I just went forward in youth camp because my friends did. That's why I always made excuses not to be baptized."

Mercedes' eyes stung with tears she would not shed yet, and across the table from her, Annette stretched her arm out to grasp her daughter's hand. "I know, Lacey. But I kept praying that someday you would believe for real."

Now, a tear raced down Lacey's cheek, and she took a swipe at it with the back of her hand. "You don't know other things about me. Rick, he promised me we'd get married, and now—he married someone else, and I'm just—no better than leftovers!"

The tears fell now in earnest, and Lacey covered her mouth to keep from wailing. Mercedes whispered to Annette that she would go get tissues, and Annette rose from her chair to hug Lacey.

"I know. It hurts too much to put into words," Annette said, soothing her daughter and stroking her hair. "It's time to get this grief all out and start healing, Lacey. Jesus is waiting on you, and he has a bright future ahead that you can't even imagine right now."

Mercedes rushed into the kitchen to ask Margie where the tissue box was. She hoped it was full, since Lacey had not yet let herself grieve for her lost love, her lost expectations, and her lost innocence.

Mercedes sat in the beautiful seashell-themed dining room with her head bowed in silent prayer. Her heart ached for Annette and Lacey, who were having private time together in Lacey's room in the aftermath of Lacey's confession and grief. This moment in time was important to be in prayer for them, especially for Lacey to surrender her life to Jesus for salvation. If that was the only reason she was here in these unsettling circumstances with this family, then she counted it to be a privilege.

Jesus, surround the believers in this house with your protection and guide us about what is happening. You allowed it for a reason, like the situations in the Bible. Like with Job, when you knew he would endure his unimaginable trial and come through praising you. Help each of us grow in truth through this mystery and gain a foundation stone we need in our future service to you. Bring the dark deeds of the past into your cleansing light. If it's your will, bring healing from any brokenness that lingers from the past, and neutralize any plans of the enemy to bring harm and division to this family. Show me what you want me to pray about this or what to do if you choose to use my efforts in your will. Amen.

Loud conversation rose over the clatter of tools being used in the foyer, making it difficult for Mercedes to concentrate. Her awareness of the impending investigation of the black cabinet across the hall made her uneasy. Little wonder the file on her work tablet lay open on the beautiful dining room table to the forms still left unfilled for Seashell Cottage.

"May I help you?" Mercedes heard Cowboy ask someone from his station at the front door, where the locksmith and handyman were finishing up and planning to go to the back door. *What now?* She wondered.

"The car park is at the limit, so I left mine in a spot across the street and walked over," said a familiar voice with a hybrid British American accent, and her heart jumped. "I'm Jonathan Holmwood. May I see Mercedes Ellison, please?"

Mercedes was already on her feet, grabbing at the chair to keep it from falling over in her haste. Had something bad happened to Quincy? Looking around for her phone, she realized she had left it in the kitchen with her purse.

She ran to the foyer, where Cowboy was turning to call for her, and stopped short. In her confusion, she opened her mouth, closed it, and then opened it again while stepping to the door. Searching his eyes with hers, she was almost breathless when she said, "Mr. Holmwood, is Quincy okay?"

"Please, just call me Jonathan," he said. "Quincy is fine. Did he not text you to say I was on my way here?"

"Oh," Mercedes said, pushing back her sun-kissed blonde bangs in a gesture of relief. "I went into the dining room to work, leaving my purse and phone in the kitchen. I didn't know you were coming, but I'm glad to see you. Please, come in out of the heat."

She backed up and waved him inside the large foyer. Mercedes introduced Cowboy to Jonathan as Chris Coulter, and he told Jonathan to just call him Cowboy like everyone else. Cowboy also explained they were changing door hardware and locks because of a security issue.

Jonathan looked at the shiny new lockset on the front door, then he turned to Cowboy. "Yes, I heard. I hope you don't mind that my son mentioned you had an unexpected delivery. Can we talk about it?"

Cowboy's dark brows shot up in surprise, but that was the only sign this took him aback. "Of course. I need to check with the handyman and locksmith at the kitchen door first. Mercedes, will you take Jonathan into the dining room?"

Mercedes had her purse and phone when she returned to the dining room, where Quincy's father waited. She gave him a small smile. "I checked my texts and let Quincy know you've arrived. Margie, the caretaker, is coming in with tea soon. And my clients, Annette and Lacey Ladson, are freshening up and will be here in a few minutes. They—well, it's a tough day."

Jonathan nodded and studied her in his direct way, and she tried to appear calm. Quincy had soft blue eyes, expressive and kind, but his father had icy blue eyes that could look steel gray. His expression could sometimes be mistaken to be authoritative and even dismissive. Right now, it was only curious.

She tried a sincere compliment to make the most of an awkward situation. "Yesterday, when I first saw the black cabinet, I wished you and Quincy were here. I knew what some symbols on it were, but you would understand the context and function of why they appear on that piece. I'm blessed to know people who have such a rich background in genuine history and the influence it still has on us today."

He nodded with a faraway look on his face, then turned his attention back to her. "When you took this job, what attracted you to it?"

Mercedes blinked at this unexpected response. But Jonathan was not behaving out of character, and she knew he did not intend to brush off her compliment. Had anyone other than his inner circle said it, he would have made a charming and gracious response to such praise. But with friends, he was often more straightforward, and right now, she could sense an undercurrent of tension beneath his otherwise suave demeanor. Was Jonathan just eager to see the black cabinet?

She wished Margie would rescue her by walking in with tea. She once felt completely at ease with Jonathan, having known his family since childhood. Then one day, she was with a group of people who got knocked down in an unexplainable incident in Peru, and Jonathan demanded that she promise not to tell Quincy she heard something the others had not. She had thought it was all behind her until she faced a resolution to that unexplainable event at her last job.

He was waiting on her response, so she cleared her throat and said, "I ran the details of my client's request through the same filters I have for any job, and I prayed about whether it was an opportunity the Lord wanted for me. When it passed through my filters, I considered it because of the unique beauty of the property. It was also only half an hour from the summer cottage in Bluffton, so I thought I would finish in a day. Yesterday."

Jonathan nodded and sighed. "You had no gut feeling that it would turn out this way."

"No! No, not at all," she said, taken aback. Her anger flashed at what she thought he was insinuating. This attitude about her life was coming between her and Quincy, and they wanted to overcome this with his family before getting married.

"Do you think I choose my clients based on whether I have a woo-woo feeling about the job, Jonathan? That I go looking for trouble?"

At that moment, Margie walked in with a tray loaded with a beautiful tea set and a warm welcome for Jonathan. If she had overheard Mercedes' vehement response, she ignored it. Jonathan's brows shot up in surprise as he locked eyes with Mercedes. Then Annette and Lacey came in. Lacey's swollen eyes were pink-rimmed, and her face still showed a fading flush.

Jonathan collected himself and rose from his seat to acknowledge all the introductions, then apologized for his intrusion. Tanned and handsome, Jonathan had a well-traveled air and sprinkles of gray in his dark hair that gave him a distinguished look. Adding his British accent and charm put them at ease.

Mercedes was certain she detected a change in both Lacey and her mother. Both were relaxed now. Cowboy came through the door, accepting the last fragile porcelain cup of tea and finishing it with two swallows. He told them that the workmen would see themselves out the back way when they finished with the kitchen door lock.

Then he looked at Jonathan. "I take it you're here about the black cabinet," he said.

All eyes went to Jonathan. He nodded, then said, "Yes. And now that I'm here, I don't know where to begin."

Chapter 9

The beautiful dining room at Seashell Cottage was still. Mercedes had been admiring the shells sculpted into the fireplace design or looking at the art in the room to avoid meeting Quincy's father's eyes. Her indignation toward his question lingered, but she was not one to clutch at hard feelings. After all, Jonathan was here to help.

The table was full, with everyone seated and waiting to see what would happen. Jonathan took a deep breath, then he turned to Annette.

"Mrs. Ladson, your brother, Anthony, contacted me when he was in college," he began, leaning forward with his forearms on the dining room table. He clasped his hands. "Anthony was rather cryptic, and all he revealed about his identity was his first name," Jonathan said. "I was uncertain if he was using an alias, which put me on guard. But since he was asking me about research I had published in the fields of history and archaeology, I thought he had information."

Cowboy leaned forward eagerly. "You were the one he found? He never revealed his source."

Jonathan's brows shot up and he turned a quizzical look at Cowboy. "Source?"

Cowboy nodded, leaning forward at the table as Jonathan was. "I was Anthony's closest friend, but after we went to different colleges, we only talked over the phone, on breaks, or on visits. Sometimes he shared a few things he was learning about his past, especially if it was public knowledge. He told me once that he came across someone who knew about a cabinet that he believed was what Annette saw. She was so young that day, only about ten years old, but he was older, and he wrote everything she said about it in a notebook he kept. He knew it was not something his father had purchased. So, it was always in his mind when he looked through history and antique books or auction flyers."

Jonathan glanced at Annette and Lacey. "Oh, I see. Yes, that would make me a source, since he found my article and then contacted me."

He unclasped his hands and sat back in his chair with a slight scowl. "When Anthony first got in touch with me, he asked me if I was certain that there had been three such cabinets made. He said he knew where one of them was."

Jonathan shook his head. "I was skeptical that a man who wouldn't give me his entire name was telling me the truth. And considering the people who owned these three cabinets, I wanted to stick with the research anyone could track down, nothing secretive. So, I asked if he was referring to the two reported to be destroyed in mysterious fires in Europe and Egypt, or if he knew where the one in America was. He told me the one in America was in Washington, DC, and that he believed the other two were safe."

Annette gasped, wide-eyed, and clapped her hand to her mouth. She dragged her eyes off Jonathan and locked them on Cowboy.

Lacey reached for her mother's hand and gripped it. On the other side of her, Margie made an indistinct sound in her throat and reached out to pat Annette's back.

Jonathan's face softened, and he kept his voice low as he said, "I had not revealed that I suspected all he told me from my research. But I believed the cabinet in DC was deep in the lodge of a secret society or tucked away in plain sight with an agency influenced by its highest ranks. Unless he was in it, he couldn't know this."

"Anthony was not a member of one of these societies," Cowboy said flatly. "He couldn't have seen the cabinet himself."

Jonathan nodded. "I believed him once I asked him point blank. He said no, and the Lord moved me to recognize Anthony as a brother in Christ. Anthony explained that he only knew about the cabinet second hand from his sister, who saw it by accident and did not know what it was. She didn't know he was searching for information about it and never thought about it, but he wanted closure about why that incident was so devastating for his family."

Jonathan paused, glanced at Annette, then said, "In those days there were still pay phones on his college campus, and he only had a few coins for it. I offered to call him back, but he said no, he would call me. We arranged an appointment, and I was ready with information about the symbols and designs on these mysterious cabinets. I was ready to compare them to what he had. I asked him if the cabinet he knew about was in a setting where the death and afterlife symbolism was relevant. He said it was in a mortuary and funeral home. I didn't ask for an address, and he didn't offer one."

Annette whispered, "Oh, no."

"But my uncle wasn't a member, so he wasn't sharing secrets under those horrible death oaths, right?" asked Lacey. "Did he ask you to do anything about what he told you?"

"No, your uncle only wanted more information than he had about the cabinet, about why it was there," Jonathan replied. "I told him what I could, and that if I ever had a reason for noting the symbols in another article, I would keep the source anonymous."

He paused, meeting Lacey's eyes. "Unspoken between us was the knowledge that the death oaths you are asking me about extend to future generations, Lacey. I don't believe he shared anything with me that threatened the limits of his father's oath, but I'm not an insider who would know. He never told me about anything about his investigation other than the cabinet. We did not talk again, and I only learned about the car accident later. I wondered if he was the same person who contacted me, only because of his first name and that he was a college student. If he was the son of a member of a clandestine group, such tragedies are common."

They all sat in silence, with their own thoughts. Then Annette said, "Jonathan, did my brother mention a locked drawer in the cabinet?"

"As part of the description," Jonathan replied. "He confirmed that the records about the three cabinets are correct about having the locked drawers. In my research, these are called the Devil's Drawer. I hope to see this for myself today, if you will allow it."

The group at Seashell Cottage took a quick break while Cowboy checked to see about the new door locks. The ladies helped Margie clean up the teacups so she could go to a job with a catering event, though she was nervous about leaving Annette and Lacey.

They walked out with Margie to get into her car, and Mercedes took her turn for the restroom. It was the only place now to be alone. Though tired from mental and emotional stress, she felt a surge of expectant energy. Her hands trembled as she brushed her bangs back from her face.

She leaned back against the cool varnished wood of the closed door and gathered her thoughts and feelings. Was it only yesterday morning that her heart gushed with gratitude and joy for a glorious day, surrounded by the wild beauty of the coastal views? Was it yesterday that she expected an afternoon alone, enjoying lunch by the marina and the boutiques and art galleries in Beaufort?

And was it only yesterday morning when she felt excited at knowing that through the horrors of last week's job in Bluffton, Jonathan had moved much closer to accepting her as the young lady that his son wanted to marry?

In his account of talking to Anthony Ladson, Jonathan admitted the Lord had moved him to recognize Anthony as a brother in Christ. Never would she have guessed that cool, confident Jonathan Holmwood would confess to any interactions in the spiritual realm. This was a revelation that perplexed her because he was uncomfortable with the things she encountered too often this summer.

She opened her eyes to count off facts on her fingers. First, she arrived here yesterday to meet Lacey and collect information for filing forms that Annette wanted about the property. Second, she and Lacey learned a mysterious delivery of a black cabinet came when no one was supposed to have access to the house, which put Lacey in danger, and she needed Mercedes' help overnight.

Third, Cowboy prepared her to accept the existence of and the extensive reach of secret societies, especially Freemasons. He had been Anthony Ladson's best friend and had insight into the cabinet that he had not shared. Fourth, the delay in the investigation by the discovery of a second break-in and the voodoo curse or blessing on the chandelier signaled Annette to reveal her family history, with ties to Freemasons through her father. And fifth, Quincy asked for information from his father and learns he was once involved in the Ladson family tragedy.

Mercedes stared at her open hand, all fingers and her thumb extended. What else?

Oh, yes. She put up one finger on her other hand. Sixth, Jonathan might believe she chose this job because she sensed it would be a spiritual challenge. Did he think she wanted to confront evil? This was the life she was running from when she chose this career and rented the cottage in Bluffton for the summer.

Or did she misunderstand his question?

She shook her head as if to clear it, and it helped. Raising another finger, she counted seven now. They would all open the drawing-room door to confront the fact that the black cabinet was there.

Then what?

She jumped when her mobile phone alerted her to a text from Quincy. With a rush of relief to talk to him, she grabbed for the phone on the marble bathroom countertop. Then she sank to the floor, her back against the door.

Change of plans. I'm at a rest stop on I-95 and I'll be in Bluffton in about two hours. Should I drive up to Beaufort or will you be home then?

From her seat on the floor, she typed a response. *We are getting ready to go in and see the cabinet. You came home early because of me?*

In moments, he sent an answer. *Can you think of a better reason? No worries, I traded with a friend to do a computer report for him if he cleans up the trailer for me. I can also send the labels he needs from Bluffton in the morning. It's no good when I'm not with you. Like I keep saying, my best times are with you, babe.*

Tears sprang into Mercedes' eyes as she typed her response. *If only I had known before yesterday what would happen, I would have waited until you were home. So much of what I've been through this summer connects to you or your family. I don't want to work anymore for a while.*

She waited for Quincy's response, and it came a few moments later. *You know I'm glad, since I've been asking you to take a break. But will you feel the same way after a few weeks have passed?*

Mercedes sat on the tiles there on the bathroom floor, poised to type. But her fingers hesitated, lingering above the phone screen. When she responded, she knew he would laugh out loud with relief. *I plan to be too busy with you to miss my work. Weddings and honeymoons can be like that.*

Then she gave in to a gushy sentiment by posting two heart emojis and a wedding band at the end.

Cowboy, Annette, and Lacey gathered in the wide foyer with Jonathan Holmwood and Mercedes. The house was quiet in the late afternoon sun, and though the moment they had come for was at hand, no one seemed eager to open the heavy wooden sliding door to the drawing room.

Like Cowboy, Mercedes had her mobile phone out, selecting the photo feature to be ready to take pictures of the black cabinet. Quincy had been waiting all day for the photos, but now that the opportunity to take them was here, Mercedes was uncertain she even wanted to have them on her phone.

I'll delete them after sending them to Quincy, she thought. She almost shuddered at the memory of the cabinet.

Annette suddenly gripped Cowboy's arm. "I wish Anthony was here."

He gave her a reassuring look and patted her hand. "I do, too. Long ago, I promised him I would keep track of you and try to shield you and any future generations from the consequences of the past. The time he knew would come is here and we must face it. But we're not alone, Annette."

She nodded. "Sure, but—there's something in the Devil's Drawer, you know. It might be dreadful."

Lacey reached for her mother's other hand. "Friends are here to help us, and I wish Dad were here, too, but he's not related by blood. This is for me and you, Mama, and we can face this together. Like you told me this afternoon, Jesus is with us. He reverses curses."

She smiled at her mother, then tugged her forward while Cowboy took the door handle and slowly slid it back out of the way. Behind them, Jonathan stood open-mouthed at what he saw. Beside him, Mercedes felt goosebumps and heard the warning in her mind again.

Expect the unexpected from an unseen enemy.

Chapter 10

Quincy's focus must stay on the road, he knew. Yet how could he stop wondering what was happening to Mercedes and his father? And how was this going to affect his plans to win over his grandparents for his choice of Mercedes as his wife? Why was his dad connected to her two most recent jobs, and how much more did he not know about his father?

He checked to see if it was safe to pass a pickup truck with a load of things in the truck bed that jostled as if they would fly out at any moment. Now he was in a passing lane that was blocked by two tractor-trailers, side by side, as one tried to pass another. He knew there would be a long line of vehicles behind him while the truck in his lane worked on passing with a restricting speed governor.

Resigning himself to a pace much lower than the speed limit, Quincy squirmed to resettle in his seat. He let memories of Mercedes dart into his thoughts. After he had foolishly turned away from his relationship with her because he panicked at the changes her ultimatum would bring, he turned to dating a young woman totally different from her. Only for a few weeks, but upon learning of this, Mercedes gave up. Immediately, she met Zach, who wasted no time getting her to go out.

Thinking of this made Quincy groan. He reached for his water bottle and quickly swallowed some. It was embarrassing now that he had been so stupid. He needed time to figure out what his priorities were, and the impact of world-wide restrictions inflicted on citizens to pull the rug out from under his profession. His wake-up was too late, since Mercedes was running away from her family legacy, choosing what she imagined was a safe, boring career and a possible future with a man who would have the same.

The tractor-trailer in his lane finally made the pass and moved into the outer lane, so Quincy was watchful of the shifting traffic and increasing speed. By the time everyone had settled into a groove again and he set his cruise control, he checked his navigation for time left to arrive at his rented vacation cottage in Bluffton. If he could maintain the speed limit without more delays, he could be home in an hour.

Quincy let memories dart in and out of his mind like the surrounding traffic. At the beginning of the summer, he felt he had to take the job in an antiquities theft investigation that connected to the Ellison family's past. He tried to warn Zach anonymously not to put Mercedes in danger.

Everything looked so different now with the benefit of hindsight.

For a few moments, no one in the foyer of Seashell Cottage moved. All eyes were on a large lacquered black cabinet, beautiful in craftsmanship but bizarre in design and decoration.

Jonathan gave a long exhale of the breath he was holding. "Mercedes, do you mind taking some photos?"

He led the group into the drawing room, and she followed him. She took a front view picture. Behind her, she heard everyone else come closer.

Mercedes moved to get side angle views for photos, and Cowboy kneeled to one knee, scanning the wood floor for any evidence of those who brought the piece into the house and photographed around it.

"They were careful not to leave any damage," Cowboy mused.

Jonathan squatted down for a closer look at the menacing clawed talons on the feet. "They were experts. Any damage on the floor means damage to this cabinet, and if this is what I think it may be, its value far exceeds the piece itself. That someone risked taking this out of hiding and exposing it to damage of theft or fire is almost incomprehensible."

"Perhaps this cabinet can take care of itself," Mercedes said in a hushed tone. "I just realized what's been bothering me since hearing Annette's story. Why place a valuable antique cabinet in a place like a mortuary? Rituals would charge a replica to use in the same way."

She hesitated, her mind racing. "Unless, of course, the mortuary was a secret meeting place, connected with tunnels so the lodge members could get there unnoticed. Pure speculation on my part, but it's said tunnels are often used in D.C., even at the government buildings."

"Of course!" hissed Jonathan, rising to his feet and running his hands through his dark hair. He turned to Cowboy. "Anthony said the other two cabinets are safe. Historical records claim that fires, set by citizens who accused the owners of witchcraft, destroyed the cabinets. Did you scan this room for wires and cameras?"

Cowboy rose and nodded. "My detector didn't pick up anything this morning."

Annette went to sit in a chair, wide-eyed, her face pale. "I never thought about the house being bugged. Or that the cabinet may have been in the mortuary because of the meetings. What in the world was my father into?"

"And what did Uncle Anthony know about it?" asked Lacey, looking around the corners of the room for any listening devices.

"I'm not sure we can ever learn what Anthony discovered," answered Cowboy. "The problem with the people behind this delivery is there is never a concrete record of facts to catch them with. They pass secrets verbally, not recording them. Maybe there were many original pieces made, maybe only one. And we can't tell if this cabinet is only a replica unless we touch it and look it over. Jonathan, would you be able to tell?"

Jonathan raised his brows and stared at the cabinet, then he nodded. "I think so, if I can see the condition of the back panel."

"Wait!" blurted Mercedes and Annette together at once. Annette had shot up from her chair and Mercedes had taken a step towards Jonathan with her arm extended.

The two women looked at each other, then Mercedes nodded. Annette turned to the men. "We can't touch this without praying first. Call me nuts or over-cautious, but I'm convinced this thing is more than wood and paint. Maybe it's the antique piece, or maybe it's a copy, we don't know. But this cabinet disturbs several of us, and I recognize that feeling as something otherworldly. Humor me, please."

Cowboy half-smiled at Annette. "No worries. You beat me saying so." Then he looked at Jonathan. "You sense it too. I watched you keep your distance from it."

Jonathan acknowledged he did, and then he looked at Mercedes. His expression told her he understood at some level the things that happened to her.

Cowboy started singing a hymn in his rich voice and they all came to stand in a circle to join him. They sang of the holiness of God, of his majesty and his name being above every name in heaven and earth.

After three songs of praise, Cowboy said, "Join hands and let's stand in front of this cabinet to pray for the Lord's protection to neutralize any evil in, on, or around it. We're going to confirm again to Jesus that we are his and we dedicate this house to Him. Evil has no sanctuary here."

Quincy passed a truck hauling a bulldozer. Bits of mud were flying off the machine's tracks, and he wanted to avoid any rocks hitting the windshield of his sports car. Once he was back in the slower lane, several vehicles ahead of the truck, he relaxed. He was getting closer to his rented cottage in Bluffton.

He wondered what was going on at Seashell Cottage in Beaufort. Was his dad resolving the unfinished business he mentioned having? How was Mercedes dealing with having his dad there? And, of course, were they safe?

Whispering prayers for their protection and for the reason for the black cabinet to be revealed, Quincy felt an odd closeness to them, though he was miles away. Prayer was like that, he knew. And a sudden surging confidence filled him that good was going to come from this incident.

Cowboy was the first to touch the black cabinet.

While his hand rested at the top corner, Jonathan put his own on the other side. They locked eyes.

Lacey exhaled in relief. "I'm uncertain what I expected to happen when anyone touched that thing, but I'm glad no one fell over dead and nothing exploded."

Mercedes stood rooted to the hardwood floor. She was unafraid—the threatening vibe was gone from the cabinet, except for the death and afterlife meanings behind the symbols on it. But she expected more to come.

"Shall we try sliding one side forward to get a look at the back panel, or try opening the doors first?" Cowboy asked Jonathan.

"The back panel," said Jonathan. He nodded to Cowboy to push his side forward while he kept his corner stable. It did not tip, and the cabinet slid more easily than expected.

"There must be wide furniture gliders attached under the feet—uh, claws of this thing," Cowboy said. "Is this far enough?"

Jonathan came around to his side, and he and Cowboy stood looking at the back of the cabinet. The archaeologist examined the seams and joints in the wood and the marks where the antique planer tools had worked to smooth the panel.

"If this is not one original, an artisan took great pains to get as many details the same," Jonathan announced. "I believe it is original work. Let's open it from the front."

Mercedes took a photo as the men opened the main doors to reveal slots, shelves, and drawers. These were painted black on the outside. The inside showed no musty trace of age and was clean.

Jonathan pulled one drawer open, and it was empty. There was no lining, and he inspected the bare wood, seams, and joints. The second drawer was the same.

Scowling, he closed the main doors. "There's no key inside for the locked drawer. If it's here, it must be underneath or on the top."

Annette said, "Jonathan, as you opened the doors, I detected a trace odor of a preservative. I don't know if it is from the varnished finish on the cabinet or from the mortuary."

"It could be coming from the Devil's Drawer," said Mercedes. "A witch had a key many years ago. But if it contains a message for Lacey, why make it difficult? Maybe it's open."

Annette gasped and her hand shot up and covered her mouth. She looked at Lacey, who nodded sadly. "Mama, you insisted there is a message for us in the Devil's Drawer. Considering where you saw it for the only time, I have wondered all along about the worst thing that could happen. A preservative, even formaldehyde, wouldn't be a surprise, would it?"

Mercedes felt the vibration of her phone and the notification tone that told her Quincy was reaching out with a text message. The group was discussing opening the drawer, so she glanced at the screen. He wanted an update.

She typed a quick response. *Just considering whether to try it without having a key. There's a faint odor of a preservative like formaldehyde. The cabinet seems to be the real deal.*

The text came back in an instant. *I'm half an hour away. I will be there.*

Thank you! She responded.

Annette squared her shoulders. "Okay. Let's try the drawer without a key. I'm ready now."

But a ring on the doorbell made everyone freeze. The bell rang again.

Mercedes moved toward the foyer. "I'll get it."

When she opened the front door, a young girl stood there, perhaps twelve years old. The girl looked apprehensive, and her big brown eyes went up behind Mercedes to see the chandelier.

Mercedes guessed she was looking for the root token. She said hello and asked if she could help the visitor.

"I just wanted to tell y'all I'll be on the porch prayin', if that's okay," said the girl, turning her attention back to Mercedes. "I didn't want no one callin' police that I was hangin' around."

Taken aback, Mercedes studied the girl. "Oh. Thank you for telling us. So, you're a Christian? How did you know we needed prayer?"

"I saw the cat witch here yesterday, after you left," the girl replied, and she tossed her thick pigtails over her slender shoulder. "And my brother saw a delivery truck here a couple of nights ago, on his way home from work on his bike. No one should be here when Margie ain't."

Cowboy was behind Mercedes now, and she moved to the side so he could join them. "What's your name?" he asked the girl.

She looked him over and seemed to come to a decision about telling him her name. "Janie," she said. "I walk by here some when I go up the road to the store." She pointed at Mercedes. "I saw her here yesterday."

Cowboy nodded approvingly at the explanation for the onlooker Mercedes saw as she and Lacey left the house. "You say you saw a woman here after the ladies left? Why did you call her a cat witch? And how did she get in?"

The girl looked at the door and frowned. "There was a different door lock then. From the bushes where I hid, it looked like a key was stuck in it and she just came inside. She's not from here and she looks like a cat, only old, with white hair. But before that, she was lookin' around the door out here on the porch to hide somethin' and she had one of those claw sticks. I saw a root hangin' on the end, and when the door was open, she stopped and hung it on that fancy light."

Cowboy nodded. "Do you know her, Janie?"

"Oh, no, sir," the girl said, shaking her head. "But I know she's a witch. She made me feel creepy, like my hair was standin' up on my neck."

Lacey was now at the door, and she drew a sharp breath. "Did you say the witch looked like a cat?"

Mercedes stepped back and pulled Lacey to the front door. The girl nodded cautiously, eyeing Lacey. "You the lady who's gonna live here now? Margie told me."

"Yes, I'm Lacey Ladson. It's nice to meet you, Janie. About the witch who was here. Did she have a car?"

Janie nodded. "A big black one with a tag from Virginia. It looked like it cost a lot. Not a person who needs to get roots."

Mercedes bit her lip and turned her head to keep from laughing. Cowboy said, "Janie, if I gave you some paper and a pencil, could you draw what you remember about the witch and her car?"

Janie pushed stray strands of hair from her forehead and nodded. "I can do that while I sit out here and pray, if you like. Can I have some water?"

By the time Annette met Janie and Mercedes had brought her a frosty glass of lemonade and a strawberry cupcake, Janie was settled into a big chair with palm leaf cushions in it. Because of the cabinet, they did not offer to bring her inside, and she did not ask. Janie shared what she recalled about seeing the witch.

Mercedes put the snack for Janie on a wicker side table, then she heard a vehicle slowing in front of Seashell Cottage. Turning, her heart leaped when she saw Quincy's handsome Mercedes convertible glide into the space where the handyman's truck had been in the last place to park.

She wanted to run to him, but she checked herself. His father was there, and other people were watching. She announced it was Quincy, and she left the porch to greet him.

The closer Mercedes came to Quincy, the more it seemed like getting to him happened in slow motion. Then his embrace enveloped her. He whispered into her hair near her ear. "It's okay, I'm here now."

She whispered her love for him and wished that slow motion time warp to happen now. But there was work left to do, people who depended on them, and so she said, "I'm glad you're here."

"What's happening? Why is everyone on the porch?" he asked in a voice for their ears only.

Reluctantly, Mercedes pulled back from his embrace. "Just as we were going to open the Devil's Drawer, a young lady rang the doorbell to tell us she was praying on the porch. It's a long story, but she witnessed a witch from Virginia putting the root in the chandelier yesterday. Her brother witnessed the delivery truck here when he knew no one was home."

Quincy squinted in the late afternoon sunshine, studying the group on the porch and returning a wave of his hand to his dad. "Ok, let's get to work, Mercedes." Then he turned to look into her eyes. "Let's do our part to solve this mystery and go home. I want to be alone with you."

Once Quincy arrived, his father and Cowboy wanted his opinion on the authenticity of the black cabinet. Mercedes went inside with them, leaving Annette and Lacey with Janie as she finished her drawings and descriptions of what she saw the previous day in a notebook.

Quincy stopped at the drawing-room door to stare at the cabinet. "I know you all prayed over this before touching it, but it still has a way of dominating a room, just by the design, color, and the message on it."

Jonathan nodded. "Are you reading the hieroglyphics in order, or do you think they are only communicating the general purpose of the piece?"

"It's difficult to say, but I suspect it's a general theme," Quincy replied.

Jonathan nodded approval and went to the back of the piece again, motioning for Quincy to follow. When his son had examined the back panel, he took him around to the front and opened the doors, then the drawers behind them. Annette and Lacey were coming in again when Quincy murmured, "Lebanese cedar."

He looked up and met his dad's triumphant expression. Together, they said, "Like King Tut's tomb."

"So, wherever this came from and whoever owns it, we know no expense was spared to build it," said Cowboy, as he watched the two archaeologists. "How old is it?"

"No way to know for sure, even if we had the labs nearby to count tree rings in the wood and analyze the pollen," said Quincy. "The wood used could have been older, recycled from another piece, or it was stored, or it was from a building, even an ancient temple. Egyptians built little furniture other than small tables, stools, and such. They don't have the right trees to cut the lumber from. But the theme of this cabinet is death. The gold painted symbols and the sphinx represent the Egyptian gods of the afterlife and the underworld, but those are different depictions of one chief god."

Jonathan looked at Cowboy. "It's impossible to tell here in this room if this is one of the three matching cabinets I researched, or if it is the exact one Annette saw, but the theme and descriptions fit all the evidence."

Annette stepped up. "I'm ready to get this over with." Then she reached out to the ornate gold ring under the lock on the Devil's Drawer and pulled it.

To the surprise of everyone, the drawer glided open, and a mist rose from inside the cavity. "Dry ice," murmured Mercedes, who was ready with her camera and captured several quick photos of the moment. She knew dry ice meant something perishable was inside, and her stomach flipped over at the possibilities.

With a gasp, Annette stepped back. Beside her, Cowboy, too, took one step back, but came closer once the mist cleared. Annette took a reluctant step up to look inside, as her friend was doing. Then she made a whimpering sound in her throat before she rasped, "What is that?"

Lacey came up behind her mother to see, and she gagged. She turned away and fanned the air in front of her face. "This explains the smell."

"It's a talon," said Cowboy. "If I'm right, it's an American Bald Eagle toe and talon. Huge, but the heavy engraved member's ring fit over it. I'll have to have it tested to see if I'm right."

"My dad never mentioned a ring to me when I saw him before he died," Annette said in a small voice. "I'm certain that if he bought one, he never wore it again when he became a Christian. I believe he would have destroyed it."

"It doesn't have to be his ring, if he ever bought one," Cowboy said in a gentle tone to soothe Annette. "There are so many unknowns in the Devil's Drawer, even if it is a message. That's their way, to be cryptic, Annette. If this is a message, as you believe, and if your father renounced his oaths, this ring is just a symbol. The Bald Eagle lives in America, and it can see five times better than a human. It has huge talons and a grip like a vise on prey. And it will steal the freshly killed prey of another bird, which is why Ben Franklin said it was a bird of bad moral character."

Lacey gulped, and her eyes widened. "Freshly killed prey?" she squeaked. "Like, a dead body in a mortuary?"

Startled, Cowboy's brows shot up. "Well—yeah, you could interpret it that way. If accounts are accurate, funeral homes and mortuaries are big businesses for the members. Some brag about their membership in the history sections of their websites, as well as their generational service as deacons and leaders in local churches. There's one half an hour from here."

Lacey gasped. "They are leaders in churches?"

Cowboy gave her a grim nod. "And in seminaries. They control doctrine in most mainstream churches. That's why the Bible insists believers must know Scripture for themselves and point out false doctrine. Don't assume pastors and leadership know and teach the truth."

Jonathan was peering over Annette's shoulder into the Devil's Drawer. "From here, it looks like the eagle's talon has dried blood on it. If so, we should bag it and have an independent lab test to see if it's connected to a crime. Don't assume that the police are not corrupt in this case and that the evidence is untainted."

Lacey had shaken off her surprise, and her voice had an angry tone. "It's always about blood. Isn't that what you tried to warn me about, Cowboy? Maybe this is only the eagle's blood. This is cruel and disgusting! I hope they killed the poor thing before they cut off this talon. What is this message saying about blood?"

Quincy was the one who answered her. "Lacey, someone didn't lock this drawer. I believe that means it is an open invitation for you to join the group. The ring represents all that being a member encompasses. It includes the death oaths your grandfather swore to become a member, and what he swore that extended to his future generations. It may or may not be his own ring, and that doesn't change the message. Blood represents those generations. Mercedes tells me that your mother is a believer. "When this cabinet was delivered, were you Christian?"

Lacey looked shocked, then shook her head. She looked at the floor and whispered, "No, I was not." Then she raised her chin. "But I became one this afternoon. And I plan to start seeing a young man who is a Christian. I'm going to study the Bible and learn not to be deceived by people like the ones who sent this cabinet, even if they are in church!"

Mercedes caught her breath. Her hand flew to cover her heart, which overflowed with joy. Quincy reached for her hand and squeezed it, and she looked back at him with tear-filled eyes, remembering how Annette told her she was here for a reason. It was worth everything she endured if she was only here to pray for Lacey and see her accept Christ for her eternity.

Cowboy drew a deep sigh, then whispered a thank you to the Lord. He smiled. "Your uncle would rejoice at this news if he was here, Lacey. It makes all the difference in this situation."

Lacey returned his smile, then said, "I believe you, and I want to honor the faith my uncle had. I choose to follow my Grandie Anna's generations through my parents and their God. He is the only true one, like we sang about before opening the cabinet. The name above all names, Lord over all those who masquerade as gods, like we sang about."

Emboldened now, Lacey pointed at the open Devil's Drawer and the gristly contents. "Is a bald eagle talon representing that these people rule over Washington, DC, and, by extension, America, in this message to me? Or because my grandfather lived there and it's from his lodge? I don't care what he swore to. I will never be a part of it."

"Yes, it represents his lodge, and more," said Cowboy. "Eagles not only have better vision than a human, but their heads swivel three hundred and forty degrees around, almost completely. Your grandfather's lodge was watching and knew all about you before you arrived. I don't believe they counted on your salvation today. You broke away, Lacey, out of the cycle. You are now in the bloodline of Jesus, who covered you with his own."

Lacey put her arm around her mother's waist and gushed. "It's like what you said today, Mama. I didn't really understand, but I do now. Jesus reverses curses!"

There was a discussion afterwards about whether to call local law enforcement about the intruders who put the black cabinet in the house, the woman who used the same key to place a spell on anyone coming into the front door, and the eagle talon in the Devil's Drawer.

Annette made the final decision, looking at her friend Cowboy and saying, "I called you yesterday so law enforcement would not be involved first. There's no good reason for my family's history to be aired in public, which could have a negative impact on my daughter's life. After what I witnessed in the past with my brother's death, I have zero reason to believe that any justice would be done."

She looked around at them all. "Do whatever lab tests and anonymous research you like for the history of the cabinet and any evidence we gathered so that we can have a file ready.

However, I'm asking you not to share what happened here until we know whether the blood on the eagle talon is from a crime. I'm so sorry to ask this, but it is important to me right now."

Everyone agreed to this, and Cowboy asked what he should do with the cabinet. "I have some men ready to help me move it out and destroy it. They are reliable. Shall I text them to be on their way? We'll cover and wrap it, so they won't see it and talk."

Annette nodded. "Yes. The Lodge delivered their message. It has no power here, and no one has claimed it. Destroy it if you can."

After Jonathan, Quincy, and Mercedes said goodbye to Annette, Lacey, and Cowboy, they kept a slow pace toward the driveway. Each was mulling over the events of the day.

They lingered together at Mercedes' Jeep, where Jonathan said he would be waiting to hear what Cowboy's investigation results were. Then he asked Mercedes what she thought about the fate of the black cabinet and the Devil's Drawer.

Mercedes glanced back at the house, then met Jonathan's eyes. She saw respect and spiritual kinship there. "Having heard your research and opinion on the cabinet's authenticity, I don't believe anyone can or will destroy it. But I believe it will disappear to go back where it belongs."

Mercedes and Quincy reclined in lounge chairs pulled together, relaxing by the beautiful turquoise pool at her cottage. The water made soft sloshy slaps in the random breezes and reflected a shimmering version of a full moon overhead. Small-town sounds of slow traffic, dog walkers, couples on a romantic stroll, and coastal marsh insects surrounded them in the clinging humid air.

"I thought when we got home, I'd talk until midnight," Quincy said in a lazy tone. "But the long drive home and the encounter with the cabinet at Seashell Cottage wiped me out. There's so much I want to say about the way my dad's past affected what has happened to you the last several weeks, about your family's past unraveling into a showdown through Zach early this summer, and you coming to grips with America's past through your work at Majestic Oaks and Seashell Cottage. I want to talk about how my dad has changed, and how I believe he will sway my grandparents to be glad about our marriage. But right now, all I want to do is sit here with you, enjoying the silence. Just to be with you is enough. If I fall asleep and snore, just jab with an elbow."

Mercedes sighed, stretched, and languidly settled again in her lounge chair. "Me, too," she told him

Quincy snorted. "I don't expect to be jabbing you with my elbow. Not yet anyway. But I hope you will soon set a date when you'll always be by my side when you snore. Maybe I'll record it on my phone and blackmail you with it."

Mercedes laughed, and it felt good. To feel good again was a sign she needed a break from the events of the long summer that would end soon.

"Let's look at a calendar tomorrow. Right now, I don't want to think about what may come or what has been. It's enough to have this moment with you, and that we are content with handling all challenges together as they come. There is always tomorrow, and the next day, and the next day, to catch up and make plans. Let's clear our minds of the stress we've been through and rest tonight."

"Do you think you can sleep? I should go soon so you can get to bed," Quincy said, reaching for her hand and stroking the back of it. He lingered over the engagement ring.

She mulled over this question, recalling all the things she saw the last two days. Most would keep people awake. But the memory of the hymns of praise she sang with friends and how she had a new sister in Christ blanketed her with peace.

Mercedes' voice was dreamy when she answered Quincy. "Oh, yes. All is well with us, Quincy, and I will sleep tonight."

Wildlife chirped and sloshed in a marsh at high tide under the full moon in beautiful Beaufort, South Carolina. The earthy odor of sulfur and salt in the pluff mud wafted through the breeze. Palm trees rustled and the dripping moss on ancient oak trees swayed like couples dancing at a ball.

Then the owls stopped hooting and silence reigned in a sandy, isolated spot near the marsh. Black ashes stirred from embers that glowed in the sand and shells, then gradually swirled upward like soot from a chimney, rising toward the full moon in the night sky.

All traces of the ashes and embers rose, leaving the sand clean. A cabinet of no discernable age formed, then settled through the portal of a checkered floor during a ritual in Washington, D.C., just as a bright drop of red blood hit the black-and-white tiles.

Mercedes slept soundly, unaware that when she turned on her phone in the morning, there would be no trace of the photos she took of the black cabinet or the Devil's Drawer at Seashell Cottage. But a fleeting interruption passed through a beautiful dream she was having. It was so familiar by now it did not disturb her, and she would only remember it in the morning.

Expect the unexpected from an unseen enemy.

Did you like this novel? You can continue the adventures of Mercedes Ellison in the Strange Sands Series. Remember to help other readers by sharing your review!

If you are in a book club or have a group of friends who want to read this book, the author is available to speak to you via a video call or zoom call.

Go to the Contact information at Southern Sky Publishing or use the contact information at BookBub, YouTube, or her artist website at Pamela Poole Fine Art.

For Book Club Discussion

I interviewed Christian believers about some of their supernatural experiences and have listened to many such stories from the mission field. We should never "educate" ourselves out of believing the realities of the spiritual realm around us and the miracles we see every day. Have you had, or heard of, an experience where an encounter or outcome could only be explained as divine intervention?

I have studied about, talked to, listened to interviews, read about, and searched online sources to get a grasp of the strong presence of secret societies of many kinds in America and the world. When my Christian friends dealt with it in their own lives, I sought a simple explanation of why Christians should not swear oaths of any kind to organizations, no matter the "good" they hope to do for their communities. For a biblical view of this, see my link to Got Questions in the Resources section. It is but one of many places where you can research the Biblical view of this topic.

What do you believe about the statement, "Expect the unexpected from an unseen enemy."? Do you have any personal examples of this?

Here is a list of **Resources** for readers who enjoyed this novella series and want to investigate certain aspects of it. For Book Clubs, there is a page called **Discussion Topics** to help leaders guide conversations and glean more spiritual insight from the stories.

Stay updated with me via my fun-packed author newsletter and websites at Southern Sky Publishing[1] and Pamela Poole Fine Art[2], or join me on YouTube[3], Goodreads[4] and BookBub[5].

Resources

There are so many! This one is where I find the most helpful research material for both reliable, quick references and for in-depth Bible Study and Biblical Worldview writing.

"Should A Christian Join A Secret Society?" by Got Questions, https://www.gotquestions.org/Christian-secret-society.html

YouTube has many podcast interviews and conference presentations with the late Dr. Michael S. Heiser about the Bible, but those who want to dig deeper will discover a lot of extra material and primary sources on this scholar's main website. I highly recommend his books *Angels, Reversing Hermon, Demons, Supernatural,* and *The Unseen Realm*, and his videos on the Divine Council and Cosmic Geography:

Dr. Michael S. Heiser[6]

---

1. http://www.southernskypublishing.com

2. http://www.pamelapoole.com

3. https://www.youtube.com/channel/UC9aV3zHRlASXUUBEF7xbT9Q

4. https://www.goodreads.com/author/show/3934732.Pamela_Poole

5. https://www.bookbub.com/profile/pamela-poole

6. https://drmsh.com/

Melissa Dougherty, Christian Apologist and author of Happy Lies
Iron and Myth on YouTube with Derek Gilbert
Marginal Mysteries on YouTube with Micah Van Huss
Secret Societies – Blood Never Sleeps by Micah Van Huss

Resources About Beaufort, South Carolina
<u>Gracious Beaufort</u>, by William P. Baldwin
<u>High Sheriff of the Lowcountry</u>, by Sheriff J.E. McTeer

Resource About American Eagle
A-Z Animals, American Eagle, online website

About the Author

Inspiring Southern Ambiance

Pamela Poole writes inspirational mystery and suspense that explore the intersection of faith, history, and the unseen spiritual realm. Her stories are grounded in a clear Christian worldview and shaped by a deep respect for both historical preservation and biblical truth.

Pamela writes inspirational stories that bring together Christian faith, historic places, and hidden truths. Her novels reveal how the past can press into the present, where faith becomes essential to discernment and courage. Her characters are ordinary people facing extraordinary challenges, learning to trust Jesus when darkness threatens and answers are not easily found.

Pamela is the author of the **Strange Sands Suspense** series and the **Painter Place Saga**, blending richly detailed settings with themes of calling, obedience, redemption, and spiritual warfare. Her fiction offers clean, thought-provoking suspense designed both to engage the imagination and to encourage the heart.

When she isn't writing, Pamela enjoys research, painting in her art studio and on location along the Southern coast and making memories with her family and friends.

Readers and art enthusiasts alike can enjoy her YouTube channel[7] for painting demos and art education presentations. To enjoy the latest content, sign up for her fun-filled newsletters and follow Pamela Poole Fine Art[8] and Southern Sky Publishing[9].

---

7. https://www.youtube.com/channel/UC9aV3zHRlASXUUBEF7xbT9Q

8. https://www.pamelapoole.com/

9. https://www.southernskypublishing.com/

More Books in the Strange Sands Suspense Series

The Old Cedar Chest, Strange Sands Suspense 1
Hilton Head

An antique cedar hope chest.
A hidden document.
A century-spanning vendetta.

Mercedes never expected her great-great-grandaunt's fragile journal and a tattered manila envelope to change her life. Yet the miraculous way they came into her possession—and the unease they stir in her spirit—would give even the most hardened skeptic pause.

Before she can meet her first client or settle into what she hopes will be a quiet summer at a Lowcountry cottage, an ominous shadow stretches across her carefully planned future. Mercedes soon realizes she is the target of a vendetta that goes back more than a century. Time is running out, and survival may mean accepting a calling she never sought and a destiny bound to the legendary Ellison family.

In this heart-pounding Christian suspense novella, Mercedes must rely on more than her education and instincts. Anchored in faith and surrounded by eerie revelations, she learns God equips ordinary people to stand firm against extraordinary challenges. Filled with mystery, history, and spiritual depth, The Old Cedar Chest invites readers to consider how faith, courage, and divine purpose intersect in life's unseen battles.

The Hidden Hallway, Strange Sands Suspense 2
Savannah

An antebellum house.
A hidden hallway.
A tale of passion and revenge.

In *The Hidden Hallway*, architectural historian Mercedes Annalee Ellison faces another assignment that challenges not only her professional expertise but her spiritual resolve.

Tammy and Clayton Popplewell hired Mercedes as they registered and renovated an antebellum house in the beautiful Southern city of Savannah, Georgia. But she knows this is not the boring job she hoped for when she arrives on the first day to find the local police there. What should have been a routine assessment of aging blueprints and structural quirks takes a chilling turn when Mercedes uncovers a concealed hallway that doesn't appear on any original plans.

As Mercedes investigates the history of the property, she must rely not only on her expertise but on God's guidance to discern something hidden—and why it matters now. When neighbors seek her out with a strange Civil War Era tale of passion and revenge, she works to uncover a terrifying darkness and help her clients make the house into the inn where they dream of sharing light—before they give up and she loses the job.

The Hidden Hallway is a gripping Christian inspirational suspense novella blending history, mystery, and spiritual warfare. Set against the rich atmosphere of historic Savannah, it's a story of faith tested, dreams endangered, and the assurance that God is always present—especially where secrets hide.

The Freedom Staircase, Strange Sands Suspense 3
Charleston

An enduring Lowcountry plantation.
A legendary patriot refuge.
A last stand for freedom.

It thrilled Mercedes Ellison to be chosen to work as an architectural historian for Majestic Oaks, a plantation that endured and survived wars on American soil. The stately Georgian mansion features the Freedom Staircase, where legendary patriots stopped for refuge in their roles with the Continental Army in the American Revolution. Her client needs help to keep the plantation he inherited, which is steeped in the history of the Lowcountry of South Carolina, home of the Swamp Fox and four signers of the Declaration of Independence.

There are also some unsolved mysteries on the property. Bringing them to light will help her client, and she finds clues in a secret passage used by the patriots. But then her archenemy dies in jail, and his son watches her. The long-standing vendetta against the Ellison family that began in *The Old Cedar Chest* now escalates, and Mercedes knows the danger she faces is real, personal, and relentless. Can she make a last stand for freedom from the past that began with the murder of her ancestor on a stormy night in England?

Blending historical intrigue, Christian faith, and suspense, *The Freedom Staircase* is an inspirational story of legacy, obedience, and the courage to walk the path God sets before us, even when it leads straight through danger.

The Dark Passage, Strange Sands Suspense 4
Bluffton

Faith tested.
Purpose questioned.
Evil revealed.

Mercedes Ellison is hoping for a quiet summer as she plans her wedding—boring clients, simple renovations, no surprises. But Marlowe House is anything but ordinary.

Doran Marlowe, a former missionary guide, has spent decades traveling the world's most remote regions. His shuttered passageway and unsettling artwork hint at experiences he never fully left behind. His sister, Mary Lou, newly returned from the mission field, carries her own burdens—discouragement, doubt, and unanswered questions about her calling.

When a terrifying incident shatters the calm of the historic home, Mercedes finds herself drawn into a mystery that defies logic and explanation. The danger feels personal, spiritual, and disturbingly familiar. In *The Dark Passage*, Pamela Poole weaves a faith-filled suspense story that confronts spiritual darkness with biblical truth. This inspirational mystery asks hard questions about obedience, spiritual authority, and trusting God when the unseen world breaks into the ordinary.

The Devil's Drawer, Strange Sands Suspense 5
Beaufort, SC

An ominous oath taken for personal privilege.
An enigmatic artifact unbound by time and place.
An evil consequence for generations.

A chilling mystery unfolds at Seashell Cottage as architectural historian Mercedes Ellison stumbles upon an ominous black cabinet decorated with ancient Egyptian symbols. Delivered under the cover of darkness, this enigmatic artifact pulls her and her client into a web of secrets that stretches across generations.

As they delve deeper, a private investigator friend joins them in unraveling the sinister connection between the cabinet and a long-buried family oath to a clandestine society. With blood as the ultimate spiritual currency, they must confront the haunting legacy of a deceased ancestor whose evil choices ripple through time, binding Mercedes' client in ways they never imagined.

This gripping story is filled with suspense, intrigue, and revelations. As a Christian, Mercedes knows Jesus reverses curses. But will her client come to know this before it is too late?

In *The Devil's Drawer,* Pamela Poole weaves a faith-filled suspense story that confronts spiritual darkness with biblical truth. This inspirational mystery asks hard questions about spiritual authority and trusting God when the unseen world breaks into the ordinary.

Grab your copy today and join Mercedes on this thrilling adventure!

Coming in 2026!
The Black Hourglass, Strange Sands Suspense 6
St. Augustine

In the shadow lies the truth.

A hidden letter.
A stolen fortune.
A secret that refused to stay buried.

Quincy Holmwood thought his work in St. Augustine was over until a cryptic message from a church archivist pulled him back into a mystery from 1688. How can he resist a search for the truth left by a murdered friar about hidden evidence of a crime against the Crown, committed by a powerful group of colonial settlers of America's oldest city? The trail of clues had endured for the courageous man of a future generation who was bold enough to follow them.

With his fiancée, **Mercedes Ellison**, and a small archaeology team, Quincy races to decode symbols tied to a forgotten brotherhood whose emblem—the **black hourglass**—marks the flow of time the brotherhood believed was under their control.

The brotherhood's final heir is watching his progress.

And he never wants the past to come to light.

As accidents turn deadly, Quincy must rely on his faith and the conviction that he is the one the friar believed would someday reveal the truth.

What was hidden in darkness was never meant to stay there.

Other Books by Pamela Poole
Southern Sky Publishing[10]

The Painter Place Saga
Painter Place
Hugo
Jaguar
Landmark
3 Legends of Painter Place (short stories)
The Wind Songs of the Marsh
King's Ransom
The Castaway and the Mermaid

Southern Sky Devotional
Inspired Artistry—Embracing the Creative Calling

10. https://www.southernskypublishing.com/

www.ingramcontent.com/pod-product-compliance
Lightning Source LLC
Chambersburg PA
CBHW052148170626
46812CB00004B/1645